Adam didn't reply.

His attention was still focussed on Sam as if he might read the truth in the child's face.

As Sarah moved around the kitchen, finding what she needed to prepare Sam's meal, Adam edged closer, until she found his closeness distracting. Sam chuckled suddenly and Sarah turned to see the tall, well-built doctor playing peek-a-boo from behind the bench. Like all adults playing childish games, he looked ridiculous—so much so she had to smile.

Having pursued many careers—from schoolteaching to pig farming—with varying degrees of success and plenty of enjoyment, **Meredith Webber** seized on the arrival of a computer in her house as an excuse to turn to what had always been a secret urge—writing. As she had more doctors and nurses in the family than any other professional people, the medical romance seemed the way to go! Meredith lives on the Gold Coast of Queensland, with her husband and teenage son.

Recent titles by the same author:

MIRACLES AND MARRIAGE
WEDDING AT GOLD CREEK

ONE OF
THE FAMILY

BY
MEREDITH WEBBER

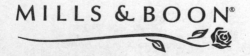

All the characters in this book have no existence outside the imagination of the author, and have no relation whatsoever to anyone bearing the same name or names. They are not even distantly inspired by any individual known or unknown to the author, and all the incidents are pure invention.

First published in Great Britain 1999
Harlequin Mills & Boon Limited,
Eton House, 18-24 Paradise Road, Richmond, Surrey TW9 1SR

© Meredith Webber 1999

ISBN 0 263 81680 X

Set in Times Roman 10½ on 11¾ pt.
03-9905-50652-D

Printed and bound in Norway
by AIT Trondheim AS, Trondheim

CHAPTER ONE

SARAH stood on the pavement and gawped—there was no other word for her open-mouthed astonishment—at the substantial building. Two floors of solid stone, restrained and elegant as an Edwardian mansion, the name of the place, FLETCHER'S SPORTS MEDICINE AND GYM, in shiny brass letters above the door.

It wasn't at all as she'd pictured it. Her image had been based on old boxing gyms portrayed in movies—places where sweat mingled with pain and success was an illusory dream. Here the dream was already realised. This place shrieked success—quietly, tastefully, but undeniably.

She turned to Sam.

'We should have gone to a hotel first, found a room—at least had a shower. We both smell, you know. You probably worse than me.'

He stared back at her, his dark blue eyes widening as they usually did when he was prepared to let her have her say. She had to smile. He was wearing pale blue jeans, rumpled and pulled out of shape from their journey, and a dark blue skivvy which made his eyes look almost navy. Beautiful, beautiful Sam!

Behind them the taxi driver finished piling their miscellany of luggage on the footpath.

'That's it, then,' he said cheerfully. 'Enjoy your stay on the Gold Coast.'

The cab door slammed, the engine revved and the vehicle moved away.

'Enjoy my stay?' Sarah mimicked. 'That's likely!'

She bent over the luggage, balancing the smaller pieces on top of the wheeled suitcase and checking the straps she'd added to hold everything in place.

'I don't suppose you'd consent…?' she suggested to Sam, and received the same blank stare, while his fingers tightened to limpet-like strength on her shoulders. 'No, I thought not!'

Dragging the case behind her, she headed towards the building. An electronically controlled door slid open. At least the place was accessible for wheeled apparatuses— or was it apparati?

Her exhausted mind fidgeted with the thought as she glanced around a spacious waiting room. The seven inhabitants, healthy-looking folk for a doctor's surgery, had turned towards the door as it opened and were now studying her and Sam with obvious interest.

Anything to relieve the tedium of waiting, Sarah decided, abandoning the luggage by the door and heading, with Sam, towards the reception counter.

'Jane's gone home and Maggie's out the back, putting her feet up,' one of the patients offered. 'We're the last for the day so she's taking a break. If you want her, you'll have to press the bell.'

Sam had found the bell and was pressing it as the man finished his explanation. And pressing it!

'Enough, Sam. She'll come when she's ready.'

Sarah waited, vibrations up and down her spine making her overly aware of seven pairs of eyes studying the two of them. Were strangers rare in this place? Did they all know each other as well as they knew Jane's and Maggie's routines? Was that why the healthy patients were making no attempt to hide their interest in two new arrivals?

Maggie's appearance halted the stream of mental questions. No wonder the woman had been putting her feet up—she looked about eleven months pregnant. Maybe twelve.

She glanced from Sarah to Sam and back to Sarah.

'May I help you? We're not a normal doctor's surgery, you know.' This brought a guffaw of laughter and some ribald definitions of 'normal' from the back stalls. 'There's a GP about half a mile down the road.'

She turned her attention to Sam again and frowned.

'I could call you a cab,' she added slowly, as if her concentration on him had taken precedence in her mind, slowing her mental processes.

'I don't need a GP,' Sarah assured her. 'I've come to see Dr Fletcher.'

'But he's a sports medicine specialist, not an ordinary doctor,' Maggie explained, still studying Sam with unabashed interest.

'I've not come as a patient,' Sarah explained, and heard a collective intake of air from the watchers in the rear. 'It's private. About Sam. Is the doctor available? I won't keep him long. Some papers he has to sign, that's all.'

Tiredness was making her stumble over her words and the fascination of the onlookers was strong enough to taste. Too intense to be activated by boredom, surely?

'You want to see Fletch? Oh, my! Oh, my! About…?' She nodded towards Sam.

'If he can spare a few minutes,' Sarah said. She was beginning to feel as if she'd walked through the door into another dimension where a gap existed between language and meaning. No wonder Alice had had trouble down the rabbit hole.

'Oh, my!'

Incredulity and disbelief battled for supremacy in Maggie's voice while her gaze remained focussed on Sam. She made no move towards the rear of the building where Dr Fletcher might be hidden, nor did she lift the receiver on the telephone to announce Sarah's presence. She simply stared at Sam, repeating the two-worded exclamation under her breath at regular intervals.

'Is he here?' Sarah demanded, going beyond tired to tetchy and impatient.

'Maggie, why are you still here? I told you to go home. I can cope with this lot—it's a group session on leg stretches. I don't know why I have to keep checking them but the blighters seem to slacken off the moment I turn my back. You get going—they don't need you to hold their collective hands.'

Adam Fletcher—for presumably it was he—erupted into the room with such vigour that Sarah blinked, yet he hadn't rushed or stormed or flung himself. He'd simply walked through a door and was there. It must be the energy he gave off, making it seem as if he'd appeared in a puff of smoke.

The focus of attention shifted to him. Without looking at the young people behind her, Sarah knew they'd all swung their heads towards the doctor. And were waiting for something! She sensed tension and anticipation in a pause more pregnant than Maggie.

Turning towards the man, she saw he was dressed as Sam was, in pale blue jeans and a darker blue skivvy. She was vaguely aware that he filled out both pieces of clothing extremely well, but her eyes were now riveted to his face—to the dark blue eyes, the high forehead softened by black curls clinging closely to his scalp.

Of course, Sam's curls were longer, still baby-soft, and Sam's nose was still a fairly formless blob, not a fine, straight, thin-ridged sculpture separating well-defined cheekbones, while Sam's mouth—

'Who are you?' he demanded—Adam Fletcher, not Sam.

'I'm Sarah Tremayne, and if you're Dr Fletcher I had to see you and I didn't have a home address so I came here.' She spoke quickly, anxious to explain before the situation deteriorated any further. 'Of course, we're both really tired and perhaps we should have gone to a hotel and had a sleep first, but it seemed important to make contact with you. Also, there's another train tonight so if I can get the business fixed up we could go back to Sydney and stay there for a while to rest up, before tackling the trip home.'

She'd done enough nursing to recognise the glazed expression in his eyes as shock so she added helpfully, 'It's Sam, you see. I need your permission to adopt him as he's officially yours—well, I suppose he is. I don't know all the legalities, but I'm assuming—m

'Officially mine?' The voice, which had sounded authoritative but kind a little earlier, was now honed to steel. 'When I've never seen either you or him before in my life?'

'Drunken orgy?' a female member of the audience offered. 'Followed by a memory lapse?'

'And to think how he lectures us on responsibility for our behaviour!' one of the young men chided.

'Maybe you donated sperm,' someone suggested above the exaggerated gasps of shock and barely muffled laughter. 'Fatherhood by remote control.'

'He looks like you,' Maggie pointed out and received a glare from her boss in reply, then another unseen contributor backed her up with, 'Dead ringer, Fletch! I don't think you'll wriggle out of this one.'

At any other time, Sarah might have smiled—perhaps even laughed—at the ribald jocularity, but Sam was getting heavy on her arm and tiredness was draping itself around her like a suffocating blanket.

'Could we sit down somewhere and discuss this?' she asked. 'If possible, without the comedy chorus.'

Her voice must have broken into his reverie for Adam Fletcher shook his head. Perhaps the physical movement was needed to return him to the present. He turned from his visual fascination with Sam, and his dark blue eyes focussed on her.

'Come into my office.' The words were spoken quietly, as if he were still caught up in a dream—or lost too deep in thought to surface properly—but as she settled Sam on her hip and prepared to follow him the energy and vigour returned and he spun, brushed past her and faced the fascinated audience.

'Maggie, you go home. Paul, you know the exercises as well as I do. Take those smart-mouths up to the gym and do a full routine—the six hamstring stretches, spine and quadriceps. Pair off so you can watch each other's technique and point out weaknesses—feet too far apart, moving too quickly—and remember you're stretching, not taking part in a flexibility competition. I'll be with you in fifteen minutes.'

Orders given, he did a sharp about-turn, dodged carefully by Sarah again and led the way down a short corridor lined with photographs of sports stars. Well, presumably they were sports stars. They gleamed with health—and possibly sweat—and most held aloft trophies of one kind or another or punched the air with clenched fists, like tribal warriors threatening their foes.

'Here, take that chair. Sit. Do you want to put the baby down?'

He spoke with a crisp authority—a man used not only to giving orders but to having them obeyed.

Sarah sat, too relieved to take the weight off her feet to argue with his peremptory manner. Sam shifted from side-clinging position to front-clinging position and settled his chubby legs around her waist, his hands clutching at her shoulders, his face burrowing into her breast.

'He'll be OK,' she said, as her host settled into a second chair and swivelled so he faced her. This was hardly the moment to explain about Sam's insecurity. In fact, if Adam Fletcher knew anything about paediatrics—and she had to assume most doctors did—he might see Sam's behaviour as a reflection on her mothering. She rested her chin on Sam's head and wondered where to begin.

Adam stared at the pair, finding it as difficult to assimilate their presence as that of the unexpected arrival of two green aliens from outer space. The child certainly looked like baby photos of himself—and, in case he hoped to deny the fact, there were eight other witnesses who'd noticed the resemblance. But what about this woman with the pale hair and serious grey eyes who was regarding him so warily? She wasn't a stunning beauty by any means and was fair, whereas he preferred women with dark hair and eyes, but she had a composure—a serenity—he found attractive even in these bizarre circumstances.

Surely he'd remember her if he'd seen her before—and he'd have to have seen her, wouldn't he? Even if it had been a drunken orgy he'd have to have noticed her—picked her out from the crowd. Were drunken orgies crowded? He couldn't recall ever having taken part in such a thing, although drinking had been an accepted social activity early in his student days...but this child wasn't old enough... Even if he had...which he hadn't...

He pushed the mish-mash of supposition and memory aside and concentrated on the woman, waiting for her to explain—certain it must be a hoax of some kind. She was after a meal ticket, or at least maintenance for the child for life. Ever since that stupid article on eligible bachelors had been published he'd had women phoning on flimsy pretexts, meeting him 'accidentally' on the beach, wanting to consult...

As he watched, suspicion making him more aware of everything about her, her eyes clouded with doubts and her lips trembled as if she was suddenly uncertain of her programme. Shouldn't a con artist have more composure? Wouldn't she have her story off pat?

'Sarah Tremayne, you said? And Sam? And adoption?' Heaven knew why he was prompting her. It would be far better if she were suddenly struck dumb and disappeared back into whatever void she'd sprung from.

Unfortunately, the prompt must have worked for she straightened in the chair, winced as the child took a firmer grip on her flesh then said quite calmly, 'I want to adopt Sam—make him legally mine. He's been mostly mine since he was born, you see, but I need to make it official, to make him family.'

Her voice, which was soft and slightly strained, cracked on the last word and he suspected she had to swallow hard before she could continue.

'I need your permission—just a letter duly authorised, my solicitor said, but I need it before I approach the welfare people because I don't think they know I've got him. In fact, I sometimes wonder if he exists at all as far as they're concerned.'

Maybe it wasn't a con job. Maybe she was mad. A

softly spoken, angelic-looking madwoman, rambling on about papers and solicitors and welfare and a baby that might not exist although his presence in the room made his non-existence unlikely. Adam wanted to dismiss her, to placate her in some manner, certainly, but then dismiss her. And the child. He wasn't into children—well, not at this size.

Perhaps he could assure her the child was legally hers even without a father's permission—then he could send her away and never see her again. The infant had stopped nuzzling at her breast and turned towards him, staring at him with his wide eyes as if waiting, like his mother, for him to speak.

'You don't need to adopt your own child, and you certainly don't need my permission for anything,' Adam began, more gently than he'd intended because, for some reason, he was battling a feeling of betrayal in that unspoken denial of relationship.

His visitor closed her eyes. Shutting out his words? Then she opened them and smiled.

'I'm sorry, I'm not doing this very well, am I? It's been such a long trip—days and days and days on the train, and no way to take a shower, with limpet here not willing to let go of me. He's had too many ear infections for me to risk flying over so it was train or nothing. I think my mind stopped working at about Broken Hill and since then I've been operating on automatic pilot. All I could think of was the journey's end, and now I've made it I'm not quite sure...'

Days and days on a train? Through Broken Hill? Coldness swept over him—coldness and the kind of fear the inexplicable brings in its wake.

'Where have you come from?' he demanded, and guessed the answer before she replied. It wasn't outer space but it might as well have been for all the contact he and his family had had with Fiona over the last two years.

'Perth,' she said, hitting the bull's-eye of his thoughts. 'Sam's Fiona's baby.'

Great! Sarah thought. As if the man wasn't sufficiently shocked by our arrival, you have to blurt the news out just like that!

'I should explain—'

'Fiona didn't have a baby!'

His no-nonsense rebuttal drowned out her words and she let her head rest on Sam's again.

'You wouldn't know,' she told him coldly. 'You'd washed your hands of her.'

Anger brushed its heat across the high, strong bones of his cheeks and Sarah knew she'd made a mistake.

'Or she of you, I suppose,' she added wearily, hoping to make amends. The last thing she'd intended had been to anger the man who held the key to her happiness in his signature. 'She never mentioned her family so I assumed—'

'We'd kicked her out?' he demanded bitterly.

Placate him, calm him down, Sarah's tired mind insisted. She took a deep breath and tried.

'She didn't talk about whatever had happened. It was as if she'd deliberately blanked out all memories of the past, although sometimes she seemed to regret—'

'Running away and leaving no intimation of where she might be going? Giving up like that when she knew how much it would hurt her mother and her gran?'

And you, Sarah added, recognising pain as well as anger in his voice.

'Addiction turns people inward, makes them selfish.'

She offered the weak excuses she herself had made for Fiona when the girl had disappeared for days on end.

'You know from experience?' The words were shot at her, shot through with suspicion as well.

'Experience of Fiona, that's all,' Sarah told him quietly. She paused, assessing the depth of the suspicion in those eerily familiar eyes, then added, 'She did the same to me. To me and Sam. She tried to reform, I know she did, when she realised she was pregnant, but it was too little too late. Then when Sam was born and he was so sick she couldn't cope. One day she just wasn't there and I knew she'd gone away. I told myself it was for my sake—and his—so we didn't have to watch the terminal stages of her illness. I believe she did it to save us pain.'

Adam Fletcher had picked up a pen and was twisting it between his fingers. As Sarah watched, those fingers stilled, tightened, their knuckles whitening.

'Her illness? OK, I know addiction is an illness, but terminal?' He growled the words at her, but the huskiness told her Fiona hadn't saved him any pain. Pain was something Fiona had taught, not eased.

'I think of addiction that way now,' Sarah murmured, rocking Sam against her as she explained a theory she'd thought long and hard to formulate. 'Like some forms of mental illness. When the victims die, those who loved them tear themselves apart, wondering what they could have done, whether they should have done more. But I now believe that death, for some, is as inevitable as the death of a patient with incurable cancer, and the families and friends of those few are just as impotent to stop the irrevocable end.'

Silence greeted her words, silence and a closer scrutiny, as if he was recataloguing her in some way.

'Sam's nine months old. I met Fiona when she was six months pregnant. She came to a pregnancy clinic I was running. She was very thin and had suffered amenorrhoea for so long she had no idea she was able to conceive a child. In fact, I suppose that in itself was a miracle.'

More silence, unyielding in its implacability. Sarah spilled her words into it.

'When the pregnancy was confirmed she changed—became serious about getting off drugs, wanted the best for the baby. She moved in with me, ate proper meals, stayed clean—or almost clean. She couldn't attempt to go cold turkey because the doctors felt such a sudden withdrawal could lead to foetal death.'

She paused, wondering how much this man might know about drug-addicted babies. His eyes, alert and aware, met hers and he nodded, not with understanding or sympathy but merely indicating she should continue.

'Unfortunately, it gave her permission—approval even—to keep using. It was legally prescribed addiction in controlled doses. But she was going to stop—intended to—after he was born. She had it all planned. It was only when she saw him—when she realised how she'd made him suffer—I think she might have—' Sarah stopped abruptly.

Enough of false hope and platitudes. If she was to have dealings with this man then let them be honest. 'No, I don't,' she contradicted herself. 'Sam's condition was the excuse she needed to stay on drugs—to seek oblivion. If he'd been a perfect child she'd have found some other excuse.'

She stared at the man Maggie had called Fletch, alarmed by her own spate of words—by hearing things she'd only thought in her blackest moments and banished quickly lest they infected the very air she'd shared with Fiona.

'But you'd know that. You and your family must have been through much the same scenario with her at some time,' she added bleakly.

'Sam's Fiona's baby?'

Great! I've poured out my guts to this man and he's back at square one—struggling to assimilate the first sentence.

'I thought doctors were supposed to be intelligent,' she muttered scathingly. 'I've his birth certificate if you want proof.'

He smiled, not a particularly nice smile—more a readjustment of his lips which gave him an irritating air of superiority.

'Oh, I'm sure you would have,' he said. 'In fact, I'm sure you've left no stone unturned.'

'Stone unturned?' Sarah stared at him, feeling her brows furrowing as she tried to make the conversational leap. 'What on earth do you mean? Not that it matters, because I'm sure you want as little to do with Sam as he wants to do with you, so how about you give me written permission to adopt him and we can be on our way?'

'That's it? Sign a paper, giving permission, and you'll ride off into the sunset? No more demands? No little messages in four, seven, ten years' time? No "Sam needs new shoes, private school fees", no claims on orthodontists for his braces?'

'Braces? Claims?' She could feel the frown etching deeper into her skin as she searched for words to make her proposition clearer to this obtuse being.

'I want to adopt him, I thought I'd made that clear. He'll be mine, not yours, so what possible claim could

I—or he—have on you? That's why I came all this way, right across the continent from one edge to the other. I didn't do it for fun—or because I thought he might enjoy an endless train ride.

'I've cared for him since he was born—he's mine. He was only released from hospital because he and Fiona would be living with me. Now I want it legalised, but if I suddenly turn up at the Children's Services Department with a child they don't know is orphaned and say I want to adopt him they'd probably take him off me—at least until they did some paperwork. I need a letter to say it's OK. Isn't that simple enough?'

It was only because she was tired that her voice was cracking. She was tougher than this—she could take care of herself. And Sam!

Adam heard the note of hysteria in his visitor's voice and wondered where the serenity had gone. Then he stopped worrying about her mental state and tried to make sense of his own thoughts. No, that was wrong because the random flashes in his brain would hardly qualify as thoughts. That's what he had to do—he had to think!

He stared at the woman, saw the grey eyes, wide with apprehension, fixed on him in a silent plea he couldn't comprehend—not fully, not in all it's implications.

Then he looked at the baby. Fiona's child? Shouldn't he feel some kinship, some tie of blood? Did genes come programmed with an ability to recognise their own kin? Of course not! It would be impossible. He tried to think, but it was as if his mind, faced with what would have to be a gigantic leap of faith, had landed in a maze and he had no idea which way was out.

'Perhaps I could find a hotel,' Sarah suggested, prompting him now. 'The taxi driver mentioned there was one nearby. It would give you time to think about this. I should have written first, explained it all, but I thought seeing you might be easier—thought you seeing me might reassure you more.'

She chuckled weakly and glanced down at herself.

'I didn't realise just how long the journey was or the toll it would take of both of us. We do brush up quite well, and I've got references with me you can check if you like.'

She might be smiling, but her nervousness was building again. He could hear it in the words that tumbled over each other and feel it in the air between them. The infant—Sam—must have felt it, too, for he moved uneasily and began to grizzle.

'If you could direct me to the hotel?' she said, her dignity sitting oddly with her dishevelled appearance. 'Is it close enough to walk or would I need a cab?'

She stood up, faltered for a moment, as if the combined weight of fatigue and the baby was too much for her, then shifted Sam and settled him on her hip, soothing him with murmured nothings. Adam could see her tiredness—or defeat—in the slump of her shoulders, and hear unhappiness in her voice.

'You can't go to a hotel. There's plenty of room at my place. I'm sorry if I haven't seemed welcoming, but it isn't every day someone walks into my life with a baby they claim is mine.'

He heard the words and recognised his voice as saying them, though why on earth he was apologising and actually offering her—them—accommodation was beyond him at the moment. Perhaps she'd refuse!

There was no refusal but a smile instead. A tired smile but enough to light up her eyes and give a hint of an elusive beauty to her pale face.

'Stirred up all kinds of speculation, didn't it? I'm sorry about that,' she said. 'Can your image take it?'

Now he found himself wanting to smile back at her. He quelled the urge for there was very little humour in the situation thus far.

'Might do it the world of good,' he replied, surprised to find he could carry on an apparently normal conversation while his mind was totally absorbed by the puzzle of the woman and the child. 'I lecture the kids so often on everything from drugs to moral values they probably think I'm the archetypal prude.'

'And are you?' she asked, the smile widening and sparkling in her eyes with silvery glints.

'That's for me to know,' he said lightly, then wished the words unsaid. In his mind he'd finished the saying— 'and for you to find out'—but he wasn't certain he wanted Sarah Tremayne to find out too much about him.

Sarah followed him out of the room and into a covered car park at the back of the building.

'The Subaru's mine,' he said, indicating a dark green wagon. 'I'm sorry I don't have a car-seat for the child but I can organise something later today. I know Maggie's got one she won't be needing until her baby grows out of the baby capsule.'

He was speaking briskly, almost brusquely, but beneath the gruff exterior he was obviously a thoughtful man. The fact registered with Sarah as she peered into the back of the wagon. He must have everything but a baby seat, and possibly the kitchen sink, she decided, seeing the gear stacked in the back. There were also roof racks on the top. For surf skis? A kayak or canoe? Was the man a sports freak? Probably, considering the line of work he'd chosen.

'I'll see my group then bring your luggage. Shouldn't be long,' he said, opening the passenger door for her.

Too weary to wonder where he'd find space for her luggage, she climbed in and settled Sam so she could put the seat belt around both of them. He was still complaining quietly so she reached into the carry-all she kept slung over her free shoulder and found a bottle of juice.

'This should hold you till we get to wherever we're going,' she told him. 'Then a bath, proper food and bed for you, mister. As soon as we reach his place.'

Sam was still sucking on the bottle when Adam Fletcher returned, sliding into the seat beside her and driving off with a minimum of fuss. No flashy showing off, just careful competence, pointing out the university, a huge shopping centre, the 'beach houses' of the older suburbs nestled in the shadows of huge new developments, interesting glimpses of the famous holiday destination as they headed east towards the shoreline.

His 'tour-guide' behaviour added to the unreality of the situation, making the drive seem like something happening in a dream where the ridiculous appeared normal, the bizarre quite acceptable.

'His place' was a melding of timber, glass and corrugated iron, fitted together to give the impression of a large colourful insect, resting on a dune above the beach.

'It's built on four levels so every room has a view of the ocean,' he explained as garage doors rose to the command of the remote control. 'On this level is the garage and rumpus room, with the living area and kitchen above then bedrooms on the two higher levels.'

Sarah struggled to release the seat belt, trying to extricate herself and Sam from the far-from-safe arrangement.

Her chauffeur came around and opened her door, then

reached inside to help her untangle baby limbs from the webbing. She felt the firmness in his hands and strength as he helped her out—not an easy task, with Sam still clinging, koala-fashion, to her chest.

A polite man as well as thoughtful, she decided, struggling to match the uncaring image of Adam Fletcher she'd carried in her mind to the very real and solid presence by her side. He ignored their luggage and ushered them towards a door.

'Here you are,' he said, leading her into a wide, glass-fronted room with overwhelming views of the beach and rolling, green-blue ocean.

'It's beautiful,' she breathed, walking towards the windows and shifting Sam so he could share the view. 'See, Sam, the beach. I told you there was a beach over here, didn't I?'

'Did he doubt you?' the man asked, and Sarah found herself smiling at the dry comment. She turned towards her host.

'Well, he's certainly been dubious about this travel business,' she replied. 'Like this clinging. At home he's a very independent little boy and crawls around the floor, playing with his toys—he's nearly walking, you know. I'm sure he would have been if he hadn't been so sick early on.'

'You mentioned—'

The shrill ringing of the phone cut off whatever he'd been going to say, and Sarah found herself being hustled across the room.

'This is the lift. Take it to the second floor—you'll find a bedroom on the left and another on the right with a bathroom in between. Decide on whichever room you like. I'll get the phone then bring your luggage in a minute.'

She was adding bossy to her mental list of his attributes when he smiled, quite unexpectedly but with the first hint of warmth she'd seen since meeting him. As the lift rose she wondered whether it had been his behaviour or that smile which had left her more bewildered.

CHAPTER TWO

ONE glimpse of the bedrooms and Sarah found she didn't care. The biggest problem was whether to take the northern room, which looked up the beach to a distant cluster of high-rise buildings which she assumed to be Surfers' Paradise, or the southern one, which again gave a sweeping view of tumbling surf, with a grass-covered headland jutting into the ocean at the far end.

'You think the north—OK,' she said to Sam, who was showing more interest in the bright covers on the beds—brilliant blue with rough representations of yellow fish and starfish patterning the material.

She sat on the bed and pried his fingers loose, hoping he might sit on the floor for a while or perhaps explore his surroundings now they were alone.

No such luck! He would sit on her knee and look up at her, but his fingers had to have a hold on her clothing—this was one kid who wasn't going anywhere unattached.

'You'll have to let go of me while I get undressed,' she told him crossly. 'You can sit and watch me, but you can't hang on, OK? If I don't have a proper shower I'll have the health police after me. And you're not much better, although you've had a few sponge baths on the way.'

He smiled as if he understood, and she felt the familiar, knee-weakening rush of love.

'Oh, Sam,' she whispered, cuddling him close and

24

breathing in the baby smell of his soft curls. 'He's not going to be difficult, is he?'

Sam said nothing so, ignoring his protests, she sat him on the floor and peeled off her clothes, then knelt to remove his layers.

'Come on, we'll save water and shower together,' she told him. 'If the train hadn't moved around so much we could have done it on the way over, but I didn't fancy dropping you down the plug-hole.'

Gurgling his agreement, he settled himself back on her hip and looked around with eyes even wider than usual at his new surroundings.

The bathroom was white, with gleaming tiles and chrome, the only colour being bright blue and yellow starfish shapes in a glass dish on the vanity bench. A clean white towelling robe hung behind the door, and fluffy white towels were stacked on one end of the bench.

'Like we've died and gone to heaven, isn't it, sweetness?' Sarah said, turning on the taps and adjusting the heat.

She showered awkwardly, but after ten minutes they were both thoroughly clean. She took an extra few minutes for sheer indulgence, with the water raining down on her head. Sam chuckled as he tried to catch the spray in his hand and transfer it to his mouth.

'Now, this is where we part company again,' she told him, as she stood on the bath mat and let the water drip off them both. 'I'll wrap you in a towel and sit you on the floor while I dry myself and get decent.' She swathed a towel around him, grabbed a starfish for him to play with and dumped him on the floor.

He opened his mouth to protest, then seemed to think better of the idea, turning his attention to the starfish instead. By the time she was dry, and had pulled on the robe and tied the belt around her waist, he had discarded the towel and was sitting naked on the bunched-up material, moving the starfish from one hand to the other and humming happily to himself.

'Good lad,' she said, pushing open the door and stepping over him. 'Now, how about you take this one step further and make your own way into the bedroom?'

He let her go, watching every step she took, then crawled forward until he was in the same room and stopped to play again.

Relief washed over Sarah. He was going to be OK. When he'd reverted to his clinging patterns on the train she'd wondered if he'd regressed, but now it seemed his behaviour had been normal for an infant surrounded by strangers in an unfamiliar—and moving—environment.

With one worry eased, the next one loomed. The room was warm but she assumed late afternoons in autumn, even in sunny Queensland, could turn chilly. She was OK in the robe—but Sam?

A light tapping from outside brought relief. That would be Adam Fletcher with her luggage. Adjusting the belt and checking she was decent in the voluminous robe, she headed towards the door. Seeing her sudden movement, Sam let out a scream of protest and launched himself after her.

Not wanting to disturb whatever other inhabitants there might be in the house, she bent and hoisted him back onto her hip, muttering rather than murmuring this time.

As the door opened it framed her, and Adam found himself staring in fascination at what could have been a modern representation of a religious image of mother and child. Perhaps it was the whiteness of the robe against the blue ocean beyond the windows or the child's naked body, pinkly healthy, on her hip.

Or was it the way her wet hair clung sleekly to her head, darker than it had been earlier, Madonna-like—emphasising the fine bone structure of her face? Or perhaps her eyes, pale, yet magnetic in their paleness, which seemed to promise that serenity he'd glimpsed earlier.

'I'm obviously losing my grip on reality,' he muttered to himself, wondering what she'd made of his silent scrutiny. In a louder, and he hoped stronger, voice, he added, 'Here's your luggage. Can we talk?'

She ushered him inside, without speaking, and waited until he'd wheeled the suitcase close to the bed. Then she knelt beside it, awkwardly undoing clasps and zips and removing the stroller strapped to one side. As she worked at it the baby clung like a monkey to the thick towelling of the robe, tugging at it so the top gaped open...

Yes, he was definitely losing his grip!

'I have to dress him but you can talk. I'm quite capable of listening at the same time.'

She snapped the words at him as though his thoughts had brushed her skin and alerted her to danger of some kind. So, for all her look of serenity, she had some spirit—this Sarah Tremayne. In fact, there could be any manner of slumbering tigers hidden beneath the cool, refined exterior.

'I don't want you to listen, I want you to talk.' He'd come up here, wanting answers, determined to find out the truth behind this woman's sudden advent into his life. Come up to be firm and cautious and hard-nosed about this situation, not fascinated by images of mother and child or beguiled by a spark of defiance.

So, get on with it, Fletch! he told himself. Be hard and tough!

'Why wasn't I informed Fiona had a baby?'

He'd tried for tough but the words emerged more gruff. Somehow the thought of Fiona with a baby made his throat go tight, while the sight of the baby himself, kicking his legs and waving his arms as he tried to avoid being clothed, didn't help matters.

'Presumably because she didn't want you to know.' His visitor kept one hand firmly on Sam as she turned her head to reply. 'Just as she didn't want you to know where she was.' She spoke bluntly, not exactly blaming but obviously suspicious the family might have let Fiona go without a struggle. If only she knew!

'Perhaps, on her optimistic days, she thought she'd tell you when she knew he'd be OK. For a time it was a toss-up whether he'd survive. Because he was addicted when he was born, withdrawn, remote, unable to settle, he was put on decreasing doses of opiates, with diazepam, fluids and electrolytes—more drugs and drips than most kids have in a lifetime. He was released at four weeks but had only been home a fortnight when he came down with whooping cough. At that stage Fiona disappeared again.'

She bent over the child once more, fastening a nappy and then manoeuvring him into a little pyjama suit printed with ungainly rabbits—or were they kangaroos? As she worked she talked to Sam in some private language of their own for he answered her with smiles and wild waving of his arms.

In every touch Adam saw her love for the child—but seeing it added to his confusion. And annoyance. He was a man who liked his life neatly ordered—he hated confusion!

'Did you see her after that?' he demanded, managing to sound more businesslike this time.

She lifted the baby, sat on the bed and settled him on her knee, before answering.

'No!'

'That's it? No? She'd gone off and left you, if your story's true, literally holding the baby? Did you make no effort to find her? Seek out people she might have known? Contact her family in case she may have decided to return home? It's obvious you had an address—even if it was my clinic.'

He started pacing to relieve his tension, back and forth in front of the windows, more frustrated than angry. Exactly as Fiona had always made him feel.

'I tried to find her later,' Sarah said, 'when Sam came out of hospital again.' She glared at him. 'Can you remember a time during your studies when all your patients weren't fit athletes? Did you ever see an already undernourished baby with whooping cough? If you haven't then pop into your local hospital some day—there's a new epidemic of it all around the country so there's sure to be at least one case in the paediatrics ward.'

The glare deepened and fury glinted in her eyes.

'And, in case you don't remember your intern days, hospitals are chronically under-staffed. They have the personnel to provide nursing services, not cuddles and security. It had taken six weeks of constant attention, of gentle touching and handling, to get Sam almost to the stage where he accepted cuddles, where he acknowledged me as a tolerable human being.

'Then suddenly he was ill and back in hospital, and I wasn't going to abandon the effort and lose what little ground we'd gained. No, I didn't go looking for Fiona. As you pointed out, I was holding the baby!'

He stopped pacing and bowed his head. He wanted to apologise, but to say he was sorry seemed inadequate. And, damn it all, he had to ask the questions—had to work out what had happened, piece together the last months of Fiona's life and the first months of this child's. If the child was, indeed, Fiona's. While he was still formulating his next move she spoke again.

'Sam needs his dinner. I've food for him but I'd like to heat it, boil some water and wash and sterilise his bottles. Is there a kitchen I could use? Could we talk later? Or tomorrow?'

Her anger had died, replaced by a tiredness that etched lines around her mouth and cast bluish shadows beneath her eyes.

'Of course, I'm sorry. Insensitive of me to be haranguing you like this. Would you like to rest? Could I get his meal and do whatever has to be done? You're probably ready for dinner yourself. I'll see to that, too.'

Sarah stared at him. He was as changeable as the wind—one minute stern and suspicious, the next making kind and practical suggestions. Don't fall for the kind version, she warned herself. Accept his offer, eat his food but stay wary.

'You feed me and I'll feed him,' she suggested. 'The kitchen?'

'Get what you need for the baby and I'll take you,' he suggested, making no move to leave the room. Well, she wasn't going to get dressed in front of him so she'd stay in the robe. Opening the carry-all, she checked she had enough jars of baby food to provide Sam with a makeshift meal. How long could a baby live on processed, pre-packaged food? she wondered, remembering the strained fruit and fresh vegetables she was used to fixing for him.

'Formula, sterilising tablets, bibs and bottles.' She muttered to herself as she made sure she had all she'd need, then handed Sam a small plastic toy from the depths of the bag and rescued the starfish before he ate the paint off it. 'I'm ready.'

She looked up to find Adam watching her, a puzzled expression on his face. Serve him right for being so suspicious, she decided as she followed him back to the small lift, where he ushered her and Sam inside.

'Shouldn't a sports medicine expert be advocating using stairs as a natural way of staying healthy?' she asked while the machine lowered them gently to the next floor.

'I use them myself, but thought you might appreciate the ride. I had lifts put in when I built the place. Many of my patients—or clients would be a better word—have physical disabilities. There's nothing like trying to carry a wheelchair-bound athlete up three flights of stairs to convince you accessibility is the way to go.'

Add sensible to his attributes, Sarah thought as the door slid quietly open, though why she was interested in any attribute beyond his ability to write his name...

Like the family room below and bedrooms above, the room they entered had a wall of glass inviting in the creamy gold and blue of sand and ocean. It had lime-treated floorboards, making them a sand-coloured off-white, and comfortable-looking lounge chairs covered with a slubby linen material in the same soft colour so the inside of the room seemed like an extension of the beach.

The kitchen was off this room, separated from it by a high bench of pale Tasmanian oak. The same timber lined the cupboard doors and the granite bench-tops picked up the colour, accenting it with splashes of a darker gold.

'Pots and pans in the drawers beneath the hotplate, crockery in the cupboards under the bar, cutlery in the top drawer—help yourself,' he offered, then he turned to Sam, eyeing him warily. 'Could I take the child? Or would he sit on the floor?'

'His name's Sam and, no, I don't think he'll sit on the floor, not right away. I'll give him time to have a look at his surroundings first.' She spoke crisply, trying to distance herself from his kindness, not wanting to complicate things by liking the man.

'Did Fiona name him?'

The question made her spin to face him.

'Of course she did. Why do you ask?'

He didn't reply, his attention still focussed on Sam as if he might read the truth of their relationship in the child's face.

As she moved around the kitchen, finding what she needed to prepare Sam's meal, Adam edged closer. His attention was directed at the baby, and while Sam might be getting used to him Sarah found his closeness distracting. Her upbringing and her recent life as prime carer for a demanding infant had made her a private person. Now this man was intruding on her space—although, physically, if anyone was intruding it was her so it was ridiculous to feel that way.

Sam chuckled suddenly and Sarah turned to see the tall, well-built doctor playing peek-a-boo from behind the bench.

Like all adults playing childish games, he looked ridiculous—so much so she had to smile. She moved so Sam could hide, then turned back so he could show himself.

'You don't make it any easier, wanting to play while I get your meal,' she told the child. 'How about the floor now you've got used to this place?'

It was a brave suggestion with a stranger in the room, but as she bent he let go willingly and settled on his nappy-padded bottom, then looked up to find this new acquaintance who seemed to understand what fun the game of peek-a-boo could be. Would he know about throw and fetch? He threw the toy and waited hopefully. Yes, the new large person had picked it up and was handing it back to him.

Throw again—further this time. See if he's going to play.

Sarah grinned as she watched him, certain of the thoughts running through his head. Darling Sam!

Starving Sam!

Sentiment was all very well, but food was more important at the moment. With neat, efficient movements she opened the jars, found bowls and emptied in the contents, then warmed them slightly in the microwave.

'OK, Sam, we haven't got a chair for you so you can eat on the floor. At least it's better than the bumpy train.'

He fought against her as she tied on a bib, wanting to play not eat. Ignoring his protests, she settled on the floor in front of him, teaspoon and bowl in hand.

'This is chicken and vegetables in case you don't recognise the taste. Made by experts to build bonny babies and full of all the vitamins, minerals and other nourishment you need.' As always he turned and smiled at the sound of her voice, opening his mouth like a little bird as the teaspoon headed towards it.

'No aeroplanes?' Adam asked, settling himself cross-legged on the floor beside her. His presence, closer now, within touching distance, had no apparent effect on Sam, but it didn't do a lot of good for Sarah's tired and jangling nerves.

She didn't want to know Fiona's brother—not as a person. And she certainly didn't want to be attracted to him—if that was what this tingly feeling was. She wanted him to sign a paper and let her go home, back to Perth, to build a life for herself and Sam.

'Only when he's very tired and cranky and doesn't want to eat,' she said stiffly. 'I don't want him confusing mealtimes with playtimes.'

'Heaven forbid!' Adam mocked her solemnly, then twisted so his face was hidden behind her back for a moment before he popped out again to say boo to Sam.

Sam waved his arms and laughed, spluttering the vitamins and minerals all over their host's floor.

'Serves you right,' Sarah said severely to Adam. 'That's why mealtimes shouldn't be confused with playtime.'

'Yes, ma'am!' he said, reaching up towards the sink and producing a paper towel. 'To show how contrite I am, I'll clean up the mess. Although...' he turned to Sam '...it was actually your fault, young man. If you hadn't laughed when we started playing that silly game I'd probably have remembered my dignity and stopped.'

Sam grinned and waved a hand at him while Sarah battled an extraordinary feeling of completeness, as if the banter had built a cocoon around them, making them a unit.

'What's happening with our dinner?' she asked, hoping to break the spell. 'Sam might be happy at the moment but I can see his eyelids drooping and any minute now he'll be demanding bed. If I could have a cup of tea and some toast I— He may not go down on his own in a strange place. And I'll have to put the mattress on the floor. I hope you don't mind, but I don't want him falling out of bed...'

About as likely as me falling over my sentences!

Adam touched her shoulder, sending heat and alarm in equal measure along the wiring of her nerves.

'You finish feeding him I'll put the mattress on the floor, then I can bring your dinner to your room so you don't have to leave him while you eat. You look as if you need something more substantial than tea and toast—unless you always have a pale, ethereal appearance?'

Pale, ethereal appearance? Her?

Did he expect a reply? She watched him stand and followed the unfolding of his body, noticing the tightening of his jeans over calf muscles, the solidity of muscle beneath the soft cotton skivvy. From verbal diarrhoea to nothing. She couldn't find the words she needed, couldn't think of anything to say, her mind grappling with the realisation that her body found this man attractive.

Why him? Why now?

She dug into the dish and pushed a spoon of beige conglomerate towards Sam's open mouth. Forget it, she told herself, shovelling the food in now. After tomorrow, after he's signed the paper, you need never see him again.

Adam was pleased to escape, taking the stairs to the guest level two at a time. He had a nasty feeling that the baby was going to prove the least of his problems. The woman might look like a pale and gentle saint, but his instinct, usually good where women were concerned, told him otherwise. Wasn't there some saying about it being the quiet ones you had to watch? And that other thing about still waters...

He was considering those hidden depths when she returned. Crouched on the floor, trying to straighten the bedding on the mattress, he looked up as Sarah entered the room. Were they going to argue again? Perhaps he should stand up so he wouldn't be at a disadvantage.

No, no arguments. In fact, a smile of approval. He stood up anyway and hovered, uncertain what to do next.

'Thanks,' she said briefly, lowering Sam to the second bed and handing him a bottle of milk—formula, Adam assumed—when he began to fuss. With the neat expertise he'd noticed earlier, she stripped the garments off his lower half, wiped the soft white skin, changed his nappy and restored the layers of clothes to their rightful places.

'OK, kid, it's bed for you,' she said quietly, slipping her hands under him and lifting him gently, still lying on his back. She moved a few paces across the room and knelt so she could slide him onto the mattress.

The child sucked noisily at the bottle but his dark eyes were fixed on the woman's face. Once on the lower mattress he seemed to snuggle his body into it, but as his eyes began to close he took one small fat hand off the bottle and clasped the material of the robe she wore.

She moved so she could sit on the floor beside the mattress, but her eyes, when she turned towards Adam, showed a deep concern.

'It's natural for him to be apprehensive,' he assured her. 'He's out of his own environment and among strangers.'

He didn't remember enough paediatric psychology to know if that was true, but he did know that if you sounded sure of yourself people were usually comforted, and for some reason comforting her seemed important.

Not that she looked too comforted but, apart from giving her a hug, there wasn't much else he could do. Giving her a hug? Now where had such a ridiculous thought sprung from? Get out of here!

'I'll fix you something to eat and bring it back,' he said, heading purposefully towards the door. 'Twenty minutes do?'

She nodded then smiled, the upward tilting of her lips pressing a dimple into her left cheek. Restraining an urge to touch the spot—to see if he could feel the tiny indentation—he left the room.

By the time he returned she was asleep, lying on the mattress on the floor, with her head pillowed on her arm and the baby tucked into the curve of her body. He stood and looked at her, wondering if he should wake her and persuade her to eat or move to the comfort of the other bed.

Then he began to wonder about other things, personal things, like who she really was, this Sarah Tremayne, and how she'd come to know Fiona—if she'd known Fiona. She seemed too prim, looked too healthy in her own pale way, to be a fellow-addict, a tearaway of any kind. In fact, lying there in the white robe—

Enough! he told himself, and closed his eyes to shut out the images his mind had been tossing up on its inner screen. He headed back to the kitchen, poured the tea into a Thermos and made some sandwiches. After covering them with cling wrap, he set this new meal on the tray and carried it back to the bedroom where he put it on a small table by the window. Turning on a lamp so she'd have some light if she woke in strange surroundings, and could see the food in case she felt hungry, he pulled a blanket over the sleeping pair, then switched off the main light and departed.

Pity his thoughts couldn't be switched off as easily.

OK, so the child had a physical resemblance to himself and Fiona, but thousands, probably millions, of babies must have black hair and blue eyes. No, Sarah Tremayne hadn't chosen him purely on the basis of a possible resemblance. She had to have known Fiona, known she was dead, to have pulled a stunt like this—if it was a stunt.

Facts, check the facts. Six-thirty here meant it was still only four-thirty in Western Australia. Would the office of the Registrar of Births, Marriages and Deaths give information over the phone? Probably not.

He raced up the stairs to his room on the next level and to the small space beside the bedroom he used as a home office. Somewhere, in a file bleakly labelled with Fiona's name, he had police reports and the name of a man quite high up in the force who'd met him and treated him with kindness and courtesy. Ben someone.

Collins! And a phone number. He dialled through, imagining the great arc of airwaves connecting him across the continent. Probably not an arc at all but sharp angles, beamed up to a satellite and back down. Angles. Was Sarah Tremayne trying some angle?

'Ben Collins!'

Great, luck was with him!

'Ben, Adam Fletcher. I—'

What should he say? Even if Sarah Tremayne was a con woman, did he want to put her in to the police?

'How can I find out if Fiona had a baby? Would you have known? Wouldn't it have shown up on her death certificate?'

'A baby? Back up a bit, mate. Let me think.'

Adam waited.

'OK, to answer some of your questions. If the baby wasn't with her and none of her so-called friends were aware of its existence then, no, there's no reason why we'd have suspected there was a child. If she'd registered him at birth with Social Security then the computers might have alerted us to the fact, but a lot of people don't realise you have to register unless they're in regular contact with social workers. And, as far as I know, Fiona wasn't receiving a pension anyway. We'd have found her through those files if she was.'

There was a pause and Adam waited, knowing Ben was probably searching his memory for any hint there might have been a child. He didn't explain that he'd made sure there was always money in Fiona's bank account—that she'd had no need to turn to the government for support.

'As you know, she wasn't identified for a few days and then only because I tracked down some of the deadbeats I thought might have known her. One of them mentioned her name was Fiona and the police computer threw up your registration of her as a missing person. That's how we got on to you.'

'And if I didn't know she had a baby, if the child hadn't been living with her, there was no reason for anyone to suspect it. Her death certificate was issued on the basis of my identification—' Adam spoke slowly, feeling his way through the recent past.

'By some clerk, simply doing his job,' Ben interrupted. 'He certainly wasn't going to make his life more complicated, by cross-checking for possible issue. What makes you think it's likely?'

Should he put Sarah Tremayne on the spot and start a possible fraud investigation or think of a believable lie?

The lie won.

'I've recently heard she was in a close relationship after she left here. It was just a thought.'

'And you're either searching for some memory or remnant of Fiona in this hypothetical baby or protecting yourself against possible claims in the future. I'd say, being a practical man, it's more likely the latter.'

'Cynic!' Adam muttered, aware both alternatives were hovering in his head. 'Just tell me how I can find out.'

'The cynicism comes with the territory,' Ben replied. 'But for you, mate, I'll check it out. How far back do you want me to look? When did she come west? When was she involved with this guy?'

'Try for a birth about six to twelve months ago,' Adam suggested. Computer records should make Ben's search easy so he didn't have to reveal too much by being precise.

'I'll get back to you,' Ben said. 'Not tonight as I've got a bit of real police stuff to do. We've got some psycho loose over here. If things have settled down I'll get one of the juniors onto it in the morning and should be able to let you know tomorrow evening your time.'

Adam thanked him and hung up. It was all he could do at the moment. Or was it? If the child proved to be Fiona's…

Mind-boggling thought! If Sam was Fiona's baby, could he give him away to this stranger? Take responsibility for the decision, without discussing it with his family? If he agreed to the adoption the child would disappear out of their lives for ever. Perhaps that would be best. At least his mother and grandmother couldn't be hurt if they didn't know the child existed. But would it be fair to them?

Hell!

Damn you, Fiona! Even from beyond the grave you're

bugging me! But he smiled as he thought of his sister, remembering the baby he'd adored, the little girl who'd followed him around, always wanting to join in his games, be one of the boys. Then the accident, his father's death and guilt too harsh for a teenager to handle.

Damn you, Fiona, he repeated gently, all the love he'd felt for her—still felt—making the words a benediction, not a curse.

CHAPTER THREE

SARAH woke, cramped, uncomfortable and disorientated, her mind a jumble of disconnected images and altered perspective.

OK, that one was easy. She was on the floor. On a mattress on the floor so perhaps it was intentional.

Slowly, the events of the previous evening began to sort themselves into order. For a start, she was at Adam Fletcher's beach-side house on the east coast of Australia so, instead of seeing the sun set over the water, here she'd see it rise.

She raised herself onto one elbow, checked the shape of Sam snuggled beneath the blanket beside her and turned towards a muted light. It was on a table by the windows and in its golden glow she could see the shape of a Thermos and perhaps some food.

Her stomach seemed to recognise the food and she slid stealthily out of bed and crept towards the table, checking her watch in the light. Five o'clock—how long had she slept? She could remember settling Sam on the mattress and not another thing. Had Adam come back with her dinner and found her already asleep? Would most men think of leaving her a snack?

She doubted it but now wasn't the time to wonder, not when there was food and—she unscrewed the lid of the Thermos and sniffed—tea. She settled into a chair beside the table and ate and drank, her eyes on the view beyond the window—the dark ocean, rolling ceaselessly up the beach, and the eastern sky, lightening imperceptibly as if the sun had sent an advance guard to paint it paler by degrees.

The figure was like a darker bit of darkness on the beach, becoming a person only as it drew closer in its pounding run along the surf's edge. As Sarah watched, the jogger stopped and bent over. Stretching or catching worms? Stretching, she decided as it straightened and headed straight towards the house, turning into a discernible male and then Adam Fletcher. He reached the point where sand and wispy dune grass gave way to mown lawn and looked up.

Knowing he must be able to see her in the lamplight, she lifted her teacup in a kind of salute—a combined thank you and good morning.

He waved his arms about, perhaps asking a question or suggesting something, then disappeared from view. Moments later a quiet tap on the door gave meaning to his arm-waving.

She opened it, but didn't stand aside to let him in. Sam had a lot of sleep to catch up on, and she rather hoped he wouldn't wake until she'd had a quick shower and dressed for the day.

'I'm sorry about last night, and thank you for the snack,' she whispered, trying not to notice how the morning run had made him sweat and how the sweat made his skin shine in the lighted hallway. Not that she was into sweaty men or ones who shone—any men, in fact.

He must have understood the need for quiet for he touched her on the arm to draw her just outside the door.

'Feel free to use the kitchen when you need it to fix his breakfast,' he said, his voice husky as he tried to quieten it. 'Then…' He hesitated as if uncertain how to phrase his next request. Demand?

Forget sweatily sleek and concentrate, she reminded herself. This is important. 'Then?' she prompted, wondering what was bothering him and how it would affect her and Sam.

'I wondered if you'd mind coming to work with me today. There's plenty of space in the gym and treatment rooms for Sam to play, and I have a very easy day on Tuesdays so I'll be able to make time for us to talk. Usually I catch up on paperwork, but today...' The words, which had started firm and decisive, trailed into uncertainty.

'But today?' she said helpfully, when it seemed as if he'd never talk again.

'I don't know what to do,' he muttered, his voice angry, as if not knowing what to do was totally foreign to him. Join the real world, friend!

'All you have to do is write a letter,' she told him. 'It's not complicated or difficult. In fact, I could type it up and then you could sign it—'

'But if Sam is Fiona's baby—' he began.

'Biologically, he is,' she told him, forgetting to be quiet as her panic grew. Surely the man wasn't going to get sentimental at this stage. 'But that's not the important issue. In actual fact, he's mine. I just want to make it legal.'

He smiled and looked slightly less confused, and far more attractive.

'In actual fact, he isn't yours,' he argued with a maddening calm. 'If he was you wouldn't be here. Now, I don't particularly want to fight about this out here in the hallway so will you come to work with me? I leave at seven-thirty. I've already cleaned out the back of the car and fitted a car-seat for Sam. OK?'

She didn't want to say yes but what choice did she

have? If she stayed here at the house or went to a hotel it would mean a day of doing nothing, a day wasted. At least if she was near him she'd be able to argue her case.

'I'll be ready,' she said, not very graciously.

And she was.

She and Sam were dressed, breakfasted—she on cereal and toast she'd purloined from his kitchen—had supplies of food, liquid refreshments, toys and spare clothes organised for the day, and were standing by the lift when he came down the steps from some level she hadn't yet been shown. Did he have a wife secreted away up there? A lover?

Sam seemed to remember him, responding to his greeting with a cherubic smile.

'I won't offer to take the child but let me take your bag,' he said, lifting its weight off her shoulder before she could protest. He staggered as if its weight was too much for him, making Sam chortle with delight, then said, 'Do you actually need all this gear for one day out?'

'Probably more than this if I want to be sure,' she told him. 'Babies aren't all smiles and laughter, you know.'

'I'm learning fast,' he said, standing back so she could enter the lift before him.

They emerged in the big room on the ground level. Through the windows she saw a parade of people of all shapes and sizes, walking purposefully along the beach.

'Morning exercise,' Adam explained. 'The pair just heading north in white shorts, shirts, tennis shoes and sunhats are my mother and grandmother. They live down the road.'

'And probably pop in whenever they feel like visiting. Does that explain the seven-thirty departure and me having to go to work with you?' Sarah said, angry with the man—and with herself for being disappointed. 'What is this? Some plot to keep me a secret? I can understand you being wary but couldn't I be consulted about it, instead of being hustled in and out like some—some prostitute?'

'Prostitutes don't usually bring their kids,' he countered, opening the door into the garage and holding it open for her. 'Now, settle Sam in his car-seat, get in yourself and I'll explain as we go. I do have a seven forty-five appointment so the departure hour was necessary more than convenient.'

Realising she'd have no explanation of his behaviour until she obeyed, she did precisely as he'd suggested. She assured Sam she'd soon be in the car with him and ignored his wails as she shut the back door of the vehicle, before climbing into the front.

'See, I'm right here,' she said to him, patting his leg to provide a physical link between them.

'You could have sat in the back with him,' Adam suggested as they drove out onto the road.

'Not with Sam,' she retorted. 'He's a slow study but once he grasps a fact it's cemented into his mind. It took ages for him to accept that I sit in the front seat of cars while his place is in the back, and I have no intention of confusing him about the issue.'

'Knows his own mind, does he?' Adam asked, taking his attention off the road long enough to shoot a smile her way.

'Does he ever!' she replied, with a smile of her own, the anger dissolving into the early morning sunshine.

She looked around with more interest than she'd been able to feel the previous afternoon, but as they drove into the covered car park at the back of his building her apprehension returned.

Why did he want her here? Or had he persuaded her to come because he wanted her out of his house? Away from the women who lived close by? That seemed more likely.

'Come on, I'll show you around,' he said, slinging the bag over his shoulder as if he carried baby gear around every day. He gave the impression that he was used to being in control of his world and a little thing like an unexpected baby wasn't going to throw *him* into confusion.

Should she keep following him? Obeying his orders? Or was it time to take a stand?

'*Are* you hiding us?' she demanded. 'And, if so, why?'

He stopped and swung to face her, waiting until she'd lifted Sam out before replying.

'Yes, to a certain extent, and I thought the why of it would be obvious. Didn't you give a thought to our reactions when you decided on this wild scheme of yours? Did you never consider how Fiona's family might feel to be told she had a child?'

Sarah heard the pain in his voice and shook her head.

'I didn't see that it could mean anything to you. After all, you'd let Fiona go. I assumed, as far as you were concerned, she'd died long before she actually did. I can understand a family reacting that way when they've lived with an addicted member for a long time. Well, I can understand it rationally but emotionally I reasoned that if it was Sam I don't know if I could do that so I thought—'

'You thought we hadn't cared about her so obviously we wouldn't care about her child!'

His voice was so cold that Sarah shivered and held Sam closer to her body.

'Not exactly, but you didn't know him, hadn't seen him grow and got to love him so I didn't think it would matter to you. I mean, I could have kept him over there for ever and not said anything, and not knowing about him wouldn't have changed your life one jot.'

'So, why didn't you?' he demanded. 'Why drag him all this way? Look at it from my side, Miss Tremayne. How would you see this stunt?'

'Stunt?'

'Isn't that what it is? Didn't you come, without writing first or phoning, because you knew this way would cause maximum disruption in my life?'

Did it seem like that to him? Sam fidgeted, no doubt disturbed by Adam's raised voice. Sarah patted him and drew in a deep breath, steadying herself before she replied.

'I came because I thought it was the right thing to do. When I tried to work out how you'd feel I decided you'd want to see the person adopting Fiona's baby—to judge for yourself if the baby seemed content.'

'Yet you spoke of getting the train back to Sydney yesterday evening, of me signing a paper and the two of you disappearing as suddenly as you'd appeared. What chance would that have given me?'

Sarah tried a smile—anything to relieve the tension of this dreadful conversation.

'Well, at least you'd know I didn't have two heads, and half an hour with Sam should prove he's healthy and quite fond of me.'

'And with those oh-so-important assurances I should have signed my sister's child away? If he is my sister's child!'

So, we're back to the big question of 'if' again! Sarah

was wondering how to convince him when a loud cry from inside the building put a stop to the argument.

'That's Maggie. There's something wrong. Stay here.'

He gave his orders crisply, hurrying to the door as he spoke.

Sarah followed more slowly. If it was an attack of some kind she might be better as a reserve—and she had to think of Sam. But Maggie's second cry was louder—of pain, not fear or terror. However pregnant Adam's nurse might be, she was now in labour by the sound of things.

Maggie was sitting on a chair behind the reception desk, clutching her stomach with one hand and grasping Adam's arm with the other. Adam was dialling a number on the phone, but his attention was on Maggie.

'But I can't have the baby today,' she wailed piteously. 'Bob's gone to the Byron Bay on a job. I can't contact him.'

'We'll find him, Maggie,' Adam assured her, then he spoke into the phone, asking for an ambulance and giving the address. 'Now, just relax. The ambulance will be here shortly. It's better to go by ambulance in case Junior arrives *en route*. More sterile surroundings.'

He glanced up as Sam blew a loud raspberry, and shrugged when he saw Sarah, standing there.

'Sorry about this. Slight emergency.'

'No worries,' she told him. 'Makes me feel right at home. Have you checked her blood pressure, pulse, listened for the foetal heartbeat, counted contractions—done anything other than phone for an ambulance so you can abdicate from any responsibility?'

He looked shocked by her questions—and bemused. What had happened to being in control? The man wasn't handling this situation too well.

'Should we do that?' he asked.

'Might be a good idea,' Sarah told him. 'What if I hold Maggie's hand and you get some doctor things?'

She moved across the room and took his place behind the desk. Finding a flat paperweight which she thought might interest Sam for a few minutes, she set him down on the floor and put the shiny object in front of him.

'When did you have your first contraction?' she asked Maggie.

Maggie frowned at her.

'Of course, the woman with the baby! Are you a nurse?'

'And trained midwife so you're in good hands,' Sarah assured her. 'Now, about these contractions?'

The frown deepened and Maggie cried out again, her fingers digging into Sarah's arm as the spasm pained her.

'When I think about it they could have started last night. I kept waking up, feeling uncomfortable, with a deep-seated pain low down in my back. Then I'd go back to sleep again. I was tired—it had been a long day.'

Adam returned with a stethoscope and a sphygmo-manometer but he still looked uncertain—as if he'd forgotten how to use them or perhaps why he needed them.

'She's having a baby, that's all. It's a perfectly natural occurrence. Surely you did this in your medical course,' Sarah chided.

'Only in hospitals,' he said firmly. 'I've never had to deliver a baby in my reception area, especially one that's not due for another fortnight. Aren't first babies supposed to be late? Didn't you tell me the doctor said you had another month? And what are you doing here so early anyway, Maggie?'

'You've definitely ruined his morning,' Sarah said. 'I think he means if you'd stayed at home you could have gone into labour there on your own and not disrupted his timetable.' She set up the machine on the reception desk and wrapped the inflatable cuff around Maggie's arm.

Maggie smiled at her but answered Adam. 'Bob dropped me off as he headed south. I thought it would be good to get in early so I could get a pile of filing done—one less job for the temp to tackle.'

'Yes, well...' Adam muttered. He strode to the door and unlocked it, then returned to hover over them both again.

'Your blood pressure's OK,' Sarah said, removing the cuff and shifting the machine further down the reception desk. 'And here's the ambulance. They'll carry a foetal heart monitor and will get a more precise reading than I could without one. I'm sure you're progressing well— if somewhat quickly for a first-timer.'

'It's not the ambulance—it's Gary,' Maggie said, but the first visitor, a youth in 'surfie' gear of board shorts and a ragged T-shirt, was followed by a man in uniform, wheeling a trolley.

'Gary's my patient,' Adam added, as he moved to greet first Gary then the ambulance bearer.

Sam, sensing movement—or perhaps objecting to Adam's departure—let out a squawk. Sarah bent and picked him up.

'Such fun, and it's all ahead of you,' she said to Maggie, who grinned then grimaced as another contraction twisted her abdomen.

Adam fussed around while Maggie was settled on the wheeled stretcher, then he took her hand and bent to kiss her cheek.

'Good luck,' he said, the relief in his voice so obvious that even Gary laughed.

'But I can't do this alone,' Maggie wailed. 'Come with me, Adam. I can't manage this without Bob! With no one. Come and hold my hand.'

'You should go with her,' the bearer told him, obviously disapproving of this cavalier attitude. 'She'll need your support to do all the breathing. But you'll need to get home later so you'd best follow us to the hospital in your own car.'

Adam looked so stunned Sarah had to hide a smile.

'But I'm not— It's not— I— She's just begun—the baby won't arrive for hours. I'll get on to Bob's office. Someone must know where he's going.'

'Please come, Adam!' Maggie pleaded.

'It won't be hours,' Sarah told him more quietly. 'The contractions are too close for much delay.'

He looked at her as if she were mad.

'I can't walk out of here just like that,' he protested.

'Of course you can,' she said. 'You told me earlier you've a very easy day—"catch up on paperwork" were your exact words. If it will make you feel better I can stay on here and take phone messages or explain to people who come in. You're more worried about how you'll cope as Maggie's birthing partner and you're looking for an excuse to say no.'

Then, as if to emphasise the point that he should go, Sam waved to him—a farewell salute he was only beginning to master.

'Please, Adam,' Maggie begged, and Sarah knew they'd won.

The impressive shoulders lifted in a helpless kind of shrug and he said to Maggie, 'OK, but I take my own car. You go on ahead with the ambulance. I'll see what's booked in for today and follow as soon as possible. Where are you going? To John Flynn?'

She nodded, beamed at him and let the bearer wheel her away.

Sam also beamed at him, and even Sarah felt a smile beginning to twitch at her lips.

'Very graciously done,' she teased, and he glared at her.

'Gary, do you just need your ankle strapped?' he said, ignoring Sarah as he turned towards his patient.

'If you've time, Doc,' the young patient said, 'but if you've got to go with Maggie I can sort of do it myself. In fact, I'd be happier doing it myself 'cos Maggie really needs you now.'

'I can do an open-faced Gibney,' Sarah offered, and saw the surprise flicker across both male faces. 'I used to surf a lot but my ankles let me down and I needed a strapping which would support them but still give me flexibility.' She turned her attention to Adam. 'Why don't you check the appointment book and put phone numbers next to the names of your patients? Then, when I've finished with Gary, I can phone and explain what's happening.'

'But you—you're visiting— There's Sam—'

'Stop mumbling and get moving,' Sarah ordered. 'If you don't trust me to hold the fort you can always lock the place, put a "Back Later" sign on the door and drop Sam and me in a park on your way to the hospital. Would you prefer that?'

Did he trust her? Would it be better to shut the shop? Two more unanswerable questions to add to the muddle in his mind.

Jane's arrival made things easier—he didn't have to decide about trust or locking the door.

'Here's Jane.' Great! Now *he* was stating the obvious.

'She can show you where the strapping's kept and cancel my appointments.'

He moved towards his receptionist, explaining Maggie's sudden departure and introducing Sarah in a series of disjointed sentences.

'So I'm off,' he finished, then walked towards the front door, only remembering he was parked out the back when all three onlookers began to laugh.

'Heaven help him when his own child is about to make an appearance into the world,' Jane said, then she looked more closely at Sam, turned to Sarah, raised her eyebrows and hurried towards the reception area to take off her jacket and store her handbag in a convenient drawer.

'I'm Sarah and this is Sam, and, no, he's not Adam Fletcher's son,' Sarah told her, following so she didn't have to yell the words across the room. 'Now, I'm going to strap Gary's ankle so could you please show me where the strapping is and how to find the treatment room?'

Jane seemed startled by the announcement but led them all down a short passage, opening a door on the left.

'Strapping's in the cupboard,' she said, pointing across a treatment table towards doors built into the far wall. 'Scissors, bandages—anything you might need—are all in there.'

Gary was obviously familiar with the place as he'd followed them into the room and climbed onto the table.

Sarah thanked Jane then walked towards the cupboard and set Sam on the floor between it and the table, pulling some small toys out of her carry-all to amuse him while she worked. Opening the cupboard, she saw a neat array of strapping tape and bandages in every possible size and conformation.

'Can you hold your foot at the right angle over the end of the table or will I fix you a sling?' she asked Gary.

He seemed relieved, as if her question had convinced him she knew what she was doing.

'Fletch uses a sling,' he told her. 'That loop of gauze bandage, hanging on the cupboard door.'

She looped it over her arm then chose the tape she needed, remembering how often she'd had to perform this task for herself—cursing as she'd tried to keep her ankle still while she'd reached forward to fix the tapes. One-and-a-half-inch for the vertical strips from above his ankle, down under the heel and back up the other side and one-inch for the horizontal strips.

'How did you hurt it?' she asked, setting everything on a small wheeled tray and pushing it towards the treatment table.

'Skateboarding,' he replied 'Bit like surfing, really, because you use the same muscles in your feet and legs to control the board. Twisted it as I did a flyer.'

He had pulled off his shoe and sock, and when Sarah handed him the gauze bandage he obligingly looped it around his last three toes and held the 'rein' in his hands so his foot was pointing towards the ceiling.

Sarah cut the first strip, but before she could stick it to the edge of the tray for use later it had tangled itself around her fingers.

'Fancy forgetting that this stuff has a mind of its own when it comes to sticking to things,' she muttered, and tried again, this time anchoring the strip to the tray before she cut it. 'Does Dr Fletcher do two verticals or three?'

'Three,' Gary responded. 'You can probably see the lines on my skin.'

'Just in case I've forgotten how to do it?' Sarah joked. 'Actually, you're very brave to be sitting there at all, trusting your ankle to a total stranger.'

The lad grinned at her.

'Fletch wouldn't have agreed if he hadn't trusted you.'

No? I wouldn't bank on that. Your Fletch doesn't know me from, well, Adam! She hid a grin at the dreadful pun and carefully placed the first strip on Gary's leg. She started on the inside of his leg about six inches above the knob of his ankle, brought the tape down under his heel and back up the other side, keeping it close to—and parallel with—the Achilles tendon. The routine was so familiar she didn't need the faint marks of earlier strapping to guide her.

'OK?' she asked, as she used her hand to seal it into place.

Gary, scrutinising every move, nodded his head in approval.

Next she fixed a narrower tape, an inch wide, starting near the bottom of the big toe and running around the heel to finish at the base of the little toe. This tape was close to, and parallel with, the sole of his foot and crossed the first to help hold it in place.

'Now the second go,' she said, stepping carefully over Sam who had crawled between her legs and was pushing at the wheels of the tray.

She repeated the process, overlapping half of the original tapes with the next two. Once the third vertical was in place it was time for more cutting. The one-inch tape had to form an open-faced support all the way up the foot and ankle—longer strips at first, decreasing in size by about a half an inch each time.

When she had ten cut she began, again overlapping as she went, to put parallel straps from close to his toes, around the heel and back towards his toes, then from the front of his leg, around the ankle, continuing until she reached the top of the vertical straps.

'Feel OK?' she asked, as he released the gauze bandage and handed it back to her.

'Feels great,' he assured her. 'Well, that's me done. Are you the nurse who's taking Maggie's place while she's away? Will I see you again?'

He swung himself off the table as he spoke, then hesitated, waiting for an answer.

'No, I'm just a visitor,' she said. 'You won't see me again.'

He didn't seem unduly upset—why should he? But as Gary departed the lingering echo of the words made her feel bleak, as if her dream of she and Sam together, a real family, might not always be enough.

'Of course it will be,' she told him, and grabbed at the scissors as the tray began to topple floorwards, pulled by tiny grasping hands. 'Perhaps you'd be better wreaking havoc in the gym. Let's go and check it out.'

She was using a rowing machine while Sam crawled happily along a mechanical walking apparatus when Adam returned.

'You were right about not being away long,' he announced, as he walked in and cautiously approached Sam. 'Maggie had a fine little girl about half an hour ago. Once she had the baby in her arms I was decidedly superfluous so I came back. Jane tells me you did a neat job on the strapping.'

He sat on the floor not far from the end of the walking machine, studiously ignoring Sam but obviously trying to interest the child in his presence without causing any apprehension.

Sarah stopped rowing and studied him.

It was his move. She'd told him who she was and what she wanted—what more could she do?

He continued to study Sam, as if the child might hold some answers.

'Did you see him born? Were you with Fiona?' He spoke so quietly Sarah had to strain to listen—so as not to bother Sam or because he was fighting some emotion?

'Yes, I was there.' She waited again.

'It's different when you see it from a personal viewpoint as opposed to a purely medical one. Did you feel like that?'

So Maggie's labour had affected him in some way.

'It's very different—perhaps because you can't detach yourself from your emotions,' she suggested, and he gave up on Sam, who was edging tentatively towards him, and swung to face her.

'And now?' he demanded, almost harshly, although his voice was still only just audible. 'Can you detach yourself from your emotions and tell me what you'd do in my present situation?'

'Your present situation?' She frowned at him, perplexed by the question.

'Let's say he is Fiona's child. Would you give up your sister's child to a total stranger? Would you hide the knowledge of the child from his grandmother and great-grandmother, both of whom loved Fiona and were devastated by her death? Can I deny them the right of knowing that something of Fiona lives on? And even if I do decide to go that way, eventually, what do I know of you? What kind of monster would consent to sign away this baby's life, knowing nothing of the woman who wants to take him—even if she doesn't have two heads?'

Sarah smiled, but she knew beneath the wry attempt at humour the man was hurting. Not that she could afford to feel sorry for him. If she wanted Sam she had to be prepared to fight for him.

'The government department who arranges adoptions would check me out. They go into every imaginable detail,' she said bluntly. 'They're not going to let just anyone adopt children.'

'Which answers one question, while completely ignoring all the emotive issues in this business,' he countered, looking her straight in the eyes and daring her to put herself in his shoes.

'Everyone has to deal with their own emotions,' she retorted, stirring herself for battle.

'OK,' he said and his voice was louder—sounding in her ears like the trumpet call of a challenge. 'I'll deal with mine, Miss Tremayne, but in my own time and in my own way.'

His eyes weren't like Sam's after all. Sam's eyes could never look so hard—so implacable.

'Meaning what?'

'Meaning that while a public servant might make all the checks they like I want to know the person behind the facts and figures, no matter how well you might score on their suitability tests.'

'I'll tell you anything you want to know,' she promised rashly, then saw him smile.

It wasn't a particularly nice smile—in fact, it made her feel quite cold. She glanced instinctively towards Sam, who had overcome his insecurity enough to crawl right past Adam and was now investigating the contents of her carry-all.

'I'd prefer show to tell,' Adam said. 'In fact, I'll make a deal with you.' He glanced at Sam then turned back to Sarah. 'What if you stay here a month, perhaps six weeks? Give me a chance to get to know you—give us both the opportunity to try to sort this out—'

'A month? Six weeks? I can't believe you're serious. And what good will it do, anyway, when you're at work each day?'

'You could come with me,' he said, and his smile grew brighter. 'In fact, I could offer you a job. I was going to get a temp in for Maggie. If you're a trained nurse, as you say you are—'

'I am,' she assured him, 'but what of Sam?'

'Maggie's intending to bring her baby when she comes back to work in a couple of months. I've been encouraging her to give it a try so we've already got a playpen here and a small portable cot. She reminded me of that today.'

'You've got it all worked out,' Sarah said, not attempting to hide the bitterness in her voice. 'And after a month of this charade what will you do? Are you going to guarantee me your signature or should I be practising a bit of forgery while I'm working here and have access to your files?'

His smile switched from artificial to humorous and he chuckled, making Sam swing towards him and give a wave. But all he said was, 'You don't have to work if you'd prefer not to. I can still get an extra staff person in to help out here. I just thought if we could work together for a while it might give us an opportunity to get to know each other.'

There was another pause, this one longer and filled with an uneasy tension as his smile faded and his face grew grim.

'A good idea, don't you think? Because even if I decide to give you permission to adopt Sam there's no way on earth you'll keep me out of his life. He'll be my nephew for ever, Sarah Tremayne—if he is my nephew.'

CHAPTER FOUR

'IF HE is my nephew'? The words had an ominous ring to them, although Sam *was* Adam's nephew so, try as he might, he couldn't disprove it. But staying a month? Working for and with this man? Having him in Sam's life for ever?

Sarah wasn't sure which scenario caused her the most trepidation. If he was in Sam's life, even on the fringes, he would also be on the periphery of hers!

'I'd have to find somewhere to live,' she said, seizing on one possible area of escape.

'You will stay on with me. You didn't get the full guided tour last night, but I'm sure you noticed there's plenty of room for an extra two people.'

'"You *will* stay?"' Sarah repeated, her spine stiffening as it usually did when people started telling her what to do. 'That sounds more like an order than a request. Do you always order people around, Dr Fletcher? Do you enjoy exercising power?'

'Drop the Dr Fletcher. My name's Adam—which you surely knew if your story's got some basis in the truth.'

Of course she knew his name, although she'd noticed those around him used the more informal 'Fletch'. But calling him by his title had made him seemed more removed—from both herself and Sam.

'Don't you see it's common sense?' he continued, when she made no comment or retort. 'It means we can see more of each other. It will give Sam a chance to get used to me, and for me there's the opportunity to learn something about you. For instance, you're a nurse, but do you work? How can you support him if you don't? And what happens to him if you do?'

'I haven't been working, not for twelve months, since Fiona came to live with me, although you didn't know that when you insisted I stay. What if I had a job?'

She met his eyes, challenging him—wanting to get behind his control to the kindness she'd seen the previous evening.

'Then you'd have one strike against you if I objected to him being placed in a daycare situation every day.'

'Once I've adopted him you'll have no legal right to comment on how he's brought up,' she snapped, frightened by the 'strike' word. Then she considered what he'd said and added, 'Not that I'd put him into daycare, not regularly—not until he's old enough for kindergarten perhaps a couple of times a week. I think children do need company so perhaps a playgroup...'

She stopped. Adam Fletcher didn't want to hear her thoughts on child-rearing, but when he looked at her in that considering way, his eyes darkened by thoughts she couldn't read, she found herself babbling!

'"If" you adopt him, not "once", Miss Tremayne,' he said into the silence. 'Now, are you married? My understanding of adoption—and I know almost as much about nuclear fission—is that adoptive parents have to be married or at least in a stable relationship.'

The 'if' made her feel queasy, but she sensed the fight had just begun so she steeled her nervous stomach and headed back into the fray.

'Single people can adopt—it just takes a little more paperwork.'

'Paperwork! That's for government officials—what

about reality? Don't children need a mother and a father? What if I said I'd prefer that Sam went to a couple?'

A stab to the heart, that one! Coldness crowded into her body as blood seemed to seep from the fissures in her heart.

'You couldn't do it to me—to him,' she whispered, her voice revealing how effective his thrust had been. Then she rallied. If this man wanted a battle he'd get one. If ever loins had needed a bit of girding, it was now.

Physically stiffening her spine, she said, 'I'm the only mother Sam has ever known. To take him from me would not only be cruel and heartless but could affect him, psychologically, for the rest of his life. However, if marriage is a prerequisite for adopting him then I'll get married, Dr Fletcher.'

The man looked shocked. Sarah smiled. A small victory to the good guys.

'In fact, it would give my month working here a focus. Surely, out of all the testosterone-laden sports stars you have coming in here, I could find one who'd make a perfect dad for Sam. Healthy, athletic, focussed—'

'I'm not joking,' Adam snapped. 'In fact, it's flippant remarks like that which would make me wonder if you are the right person to care for Sam.'

She broadened her smile, but didn't think her expression was any nicer than the one he'd aimed her way earlier.

'I'm not joking either, Dr Fletcher. Marriage would be a small price to pay in order to keep Sam.'

'It's Adam, and totally preposterous,' he stormed, his raised voice making Sam spin and then head determinedly towards Sarah. But Adam diverted him, taking his car keys from his pocket and throwing them softly so they landed about a foot in front of Sam's bee-line progress.

'Your name? Oh, it's not that preposterous!' she said meekly.

It should have been her victory, but could she count it as such when the man was laughing—actually laughing out loud—when he should be slinking, cowed and beaten, out of her sight?

'Your game, but it's early in this match, Sarah Tremayne,' he conceded when he was able to talk. 'And we've strayed from the heart of this conversation, which is you staying on. Don't you consider it would be sensible? If I ask you nicely, instead of ordering you, will you agree?'

It was more than sensible—it was his right, Sarah silently conceded, but the idea seemed as fraught with danger as a pit full of crocodiles. In more ways than one! For years she'd maintained a lifestyle where men were friends or casual acquaintances, but her inner early warning system told her this man would be hard to keep in either of those categories. He was not a man you could label and tuck neatly into a file.

She searched for an excuse not to stay or at least stay somewhere else—see less of him, not more.

'Can't think of any excuse to say no? Why not give in graciously?'

Pit full of crocodiles was right. When he smiled at her like that things happened in her body which made her want to run a mile—or, better yet, back across the continent to the safety of her home.

'You're enjoying this!' Sarah said. 'Taking great delight in manipulating me—and Sam.'

His party smile became a grin of sheer mischief and enchantment.

'In some respects it has a certain piquancy. Something to do with getting just desserts!' he revealed. 'For a start there's the speculation rife among my staff and patients, which you caused, by barging in here. I think it could prove diverting to let the rumours flow for a month or so. Yes, if it weren't for the other aspects of the situation it could be tremendous fun.'

His gaze drifted to Sam, his eyes revealing the lack of 'fun' in the 'other aspects'.

Sarah, too, looked at Sam. Everything Adam said made sense and, in truth, she hadn't considered the situation from his side, before deciding to come east. But to have him in Sam's life for ever?

It would be good for Sam, she acknowledged silently. But for her?

'Well?' he demanded.

'Do I have a choice? If I want your agreement can I say no? Or is that what you want? Is this a test of my commitment to adopting Sam? No matter what inconvenience it might cause, if I'm to win your approval I have to stay?'

Sam must have heard the bitterness in her voice for he crawled towards her and reached out to clutch at her jeans. She lifted him onto her knee and held him close, forcing herself to relax so he didn't feel her tension.

'Is it inconvenient for you?'

Adam's question startled her.

'Does it matter to you if it is?'

He shrugged.

'Not particularly. If you'd put any thought into this idea before you launched yourself across a continent, you must have realised it could take time.'

His indifference stung.

'I've thought of nothing else since I discovered Fiona

was dead. That was three months ago. Sam was still sick—he had bronchitis after the whooping cough—then he was convalescing. I couldn't consider undertaking the journey until I knew he was one hundred per cent well again.'

'OK, let's back up a bit here. You said Fiona didn't speak about her family so how did you know to contact me?'

Suspicion should be his second name.

'I told you I tried to find Fiona after Sam came out of hospital the second time. There's a needle exchange programme for addicts so I went there and asked around. Someone told me she was dead so I—'

'Contacted the police for confirmation and to let them know you had her baby?'

Sarah felt embarrassment and guilt heat her body and prayed it wasn't showing as scarlet flags in her cheeks.

'No, I didn't,' she muttered. 'I went to the library and searched back issues of the local paper. Eventually I found a tiny paragraph, saying...' She faltered, the rush of emotion she'd felt at the time bringing a lump to her throat.

'It said she'd been identified by her brother, Dr Adam Fletcher, and for some reason the reporter had added you were a sports medicine specialist. After that, it was simply a matter of going through medical specialists in interstate phone books until I made a match. Fiona had mentioned Queensland so I started there.'

He was staring at her. Weighing up her story? Pondering its truth?

'You could have written to me or phoned,' he pointed out.

'And said what?' Sarah asked him. 'I have your nephew—do you want him back?'

As she spoke her arms tightened around Sam, holding him closer. He snuggled against her for a moment, then protested at the restricting embrace. She loosened her hold and let him climb back to the floor.

He moved towards Adam, then stopped halfway, turning back to look at Sarah as if seeking her permission to be friends with the man.

'I was too afraid to contact you,' she whispered, knowing there had to be honesty between them. 'I was terrified. What if you wanted him? Who wouldn't want him? I couldn't bear the thought of losing him.'

Adam heard the searing pain of truth in the words and saw the withheld tears sparkling on his visitor's lashes.

'Yet you came,' he pointed out.

'I had to.' She let the phrase slip out on a long sighing breath. 'I had to make it legal and decided it might be easier done in person.'

She lifted her head and gazed defiantly at him, daring him to disbelieve her.

He didn't disbelieve her but something flickered in his mind—an inconsistency in her statement or had it been a change in the timbre of her voice? 'I had to,' she'd said—that was it. That's what he had to follow up—one small sentence. The use of such a strong verb—'had'!

'Your swimmers are here, Fletch. Shall I let them in?' Jane interrupted his thoughts.

'Swimmers?'

'The university group you've agreed to work with during the off-season.'

'Damn, I'd forgotten all about them. Yes, show them in.' He turned back to Sarah. 'Most of our top swimmers train in the pool all year round these days, but this lot are keen amateurs rather than professionals so I'm giving them an off-season programme to improve their aerobic capacity and upper body strength. This is an introductory session. They'll be familiarising themselves with the place and I'll be checking out their individual levels of fitness.

'I'm sorry, I'd forgotten they were coming when I said I had a fairly free day, and I'd also planned on having Maggie here to do most of the work.'

Sarah turned as a group of young men and women trooped into the gym, some greeting the doctor as if he were an old friend and others looking around with interest. He'd sounded genuinely concerned and apologetic about the interruption, but she didn't want to disrupt his work—heaven forbid—when what she wanted from him was co-operation.

Besides, it might be fun to see him in action. Sports medicine was a field she knew little about from the professional angle. She'd visited such specialists as a patient, but never considered the totality of their field. Yes, she'd quite enjoy watching Adam Fletcher at work.

'OK, you lot,' he began. 'You're here to begin a programme but first we'd better have a chat about what you're going to do and why you're going to do it. Settle yourselves either on the floor or on some piece of equipment close enough to me so I don't have to shout. This is Sarah and the small person is Sam.'

So much for introductions! As Sarah acknowledged the newcomers with a smile Adam continued.

'Jake, you were here last off-season. What's your goal?'

'To maintain fitness, build strength and try to boost our aerobic—anaerobic—capacity.'

He was a tall young man, well built, and Sarah was reasonably sure he was teasing Adam with the question.

'Who knows the difference?' He flung it back at the group where a thin, lanky girl took up the challenge.

'Anaerobic enzymes drive the body for brief periods of exertion—they don't need oxygen—but for longer periods you need aerobic enzymes which need oxygen to metabolise.'

'Studying biology, are you?' Adam asked. 'You're right, of course. We can measure your aerobic capacity, by measuring the amount of oxygen you use during exercise, and give a figure of either litres of oxygen per minute or as a combined measurement with your body weight—so many millilitres per kilogram per minute. It might sound complicated but it's not and it's important you understand what's happening within your body both as you train and when you compete.'

'How do you measure aerobic capacity?' a compact young woman asked. 'Is it the same as lung capacity?'

'No, but by increasing your lung capacity you do increase your aerobic capacity. Your lung capacity is how much air you take into your lungs, while your aerobic capacity is how much oxygen you use during continual exercise. The more you exercise the more oxygen your body consumes—anywhere up to six litres per minute.

'I'll give you a graph which shows oxygen consumption of world-class athletes and notes, explaining how to test yourself, but while you're here I'll strap you up to a machine which will measure it for you. We'll do that before the programme begins—today, in fact—then again when you're finished to see if I've done you any good.'

'What about diet?' someone else asked.

Sarah watched as Sam crawled tentatively closer to Adam then, evidently feeling secure near him, turned to get a better look at the newcomers. She found herself waiting for Adam's answer, interested in spite of herself.

'We'll talk about diet and later Sarah…' he nodded towards her, daring her to turn down this task '…will weigh you all, test body fat and give you diet plans.'

He ignored a couple of ribald comments about which bits of the body Sarah might test, and continued.

'These aren't weight-loss diets but properly balanced meal plans which will provide you with the amount of calories you need to get through a regular day of study, recreation and training. You don't have to follow them or stick religiously to them if you choose to use them, but they might give you an inkling of what sensible eating is about—as opposed to simply feeding your face or quick-fix snacks of fast food.'

'Do we keep swimming?' Another young male asked the question this time.

'If you can,' Adam replied. 'Try to stick to a basic routine in the pool—intervals of up to five minutes at eighty to ninety per cent of your capacity. For those of you without access to a heated pool, or whose lecture and study times mean it's impossible, use the equipment here. I'll explain it to you later, but all the exercise you do here will mimic as closely as possible the actions you use in swimming. Isokinetic training with free weights— keep away from the Nautilus and other machines no matter how much they tempt you. The swim trolleys and swim sleds are here for your specific use.'

Swim trolleys and swim sleds? Other people repeated the words out loud and Sarah realised she'd be able to learn, without betraying her total ignorance of such devices. Some assistant she'd be if she didn't learn quickly.

Body-fat measurements she could do. Hadn't she endured sessions like these—tested her body fat regularly, eaten only what was listed on her diet sheets, even known her aerobic capacity—when she was surfing competitively?

As people scrambled to their feet and began to walk away, she realised he must be showing them the machines.

'We'd better take a look, Sam, or I'll end up jamming someone's feet or fingers in one of these things when I'm supposed to be assisting.'

She scooped him up and carried him the length of the room then, wanting to reinforce the independence he was showing, she put him down on the floor again. He looked at her and considered voicing a complaint, but the shiny silver wheel of an exercise bike took his fancy and he crawled off to investigate it more closely.

Could he harm himself on it? That was always her first thought when he set out on one of his small journeys of discovery. Some of the machines in here seemed to be designed for the express purpose of removing prying baby fingers. The bike was one. If she took on this job she'd have to introduce Sam to the playpen.

If?

She steered him towards a small trampoline, set into the floor above a custom-built well, with padding over the springs to stop even the tiniest of fingers getting caught.

'Bounce on this a while,' she told him, helping him onto the matting and setting it moving with her foot.

He crowed with delight, looking first at her and then at Adam as if to make sure his new friend wasn't missing out on the fun.

'He needs constant supervision and feeding and changing. I won't be able to work for you,' she said to Adam, who'd finished demonstrating the machines and had moved to stand beside her as he watched the students testing them.

Adam sensed regret in her voice, as if she'd enjoyed this short session with the swimmers.

'I can get someone in to keep an eye on him—and feed and change him, too. As long as he knows you're around, he seems content. All we're doing today is starting record cards for these kids. Once I've demonstrated where and how to take body-fat readings they can pair off and do each other. Jane's got the cards typed up so all you have to do is record the statistics. I'll do their aerobic capacity, blood pressure and pulse rate, show them how to take their own pulse, do a bit of exercise and then test their recovery rate.'

'Why do that?' she asked, kicking at the trampoline with her foot to keep Sam happy but definitely interested in his reply. Fitness hadn't been treated this scientifically in her surfing days.

'It keeps them interested. Training for sport is the most boring thing ever invented—it's so repetitive yet so necessary. Anything that adds interest or a challenge is good. If, after a week, they find their recovery rate is faster and their basal pulse, which they'll take each morning, is lower they'll know they're achieving something through the exercise, and that's the spur to keep them going.'

She seemed to be considering his words, a slight frown teasing at her forehead.

'But couldn't a competent gym instructor do this—or a personal trainer, a coach of some kind? Why a doctor?'

The grey eyes studied him. Did she think him a lightweight, frittering his life away playing at medicine?

'I don't spend my entire life working out training programmes or working directly with sports people, but I won't have anyone coming into one of my programmes without a full physical examination and a record of their current state of health. Exercise can be deadly if it's not undertaken sensibly. Even amateurs like these students can develop muscular or skeletal problems which will come back to haunt them in later life if they don't learn a sensible training regime and correct swimming strokes.'

'Do you do that as well? Correct things like swimming strokes?'

'Not with professionals, no, but I work with their coaches to try to change a stroke if a swimmer's problem, say with a shoulder inflammation or lower back pain, becomes chronic. Knowing how the muscle groups work and interact with each other, it's sometimes possible to pinpoint what is aggravating the inflammation.'

'You can do that here?' she demanded. 'How?'

He was amused by her suspicion but also intrigued. She seemed fascinated by the subject—one she'd probably never taken much notice of until today.

'We use the swimming trolleys and take films of the action. These are then fed through a synthesiser which has a film of what's considered the perfect action for the particular stroke. By running the two on top of each other, you can pick out where the difference is—where the strokes don't coincide.'

'Which is just the beginning, I would think.'

'Definitely. Take a breast-stroker, for example. While most swimmers suffer shoulder problems at some stage of their careers, breast-strokers are susceptible to knee damage from the snapping movement of their kick. It causes inflammation where the tendons coming down from the thigh are attached—at the pes anserinus—and the medial collateral ligament. Rest will usually cure it, but if it becomes a recurrent problem then a coach has to look at changing the swimmer's kick. If the swimmer is a champion, and still wants to be competitive, it's not as easy as it sounds.'

'No, not for someone who may have been kicking that way since childhood,' Sarah agreed, her interest piqued in spite of herself.

'OK, enough play,' Jake announced, obviously appointing himself in charge of the group. 'Let's get down to business. You ready, Fletch? How do you want to do these tests?'

He was very efficient—and probably equally effective, she realised as she watched Adam divide the group into pairs and lead them into a room beyond the gym. It had a cycling machine but that was the only familiar equipment—well, familiar for a gym. The rest wouldn't have looked out of place in an intensive care ward. Screens and monitors, electrode gel and wires and sticky terminals, myriad machines to test most bodily functions.

'Where's the cot?' she asked Adam as Sam began to grizzle. 'If I give him a bottle he'll sleep for a couple of hours and I can start work.'

She hadn't meant to say that—to give in, without gaining any concessions for herself—but she was intrigued, no, fascinated—though there was no need to tell Adam Fletcher how she felt.

'See Jane. She and Maggie were planning to use the second treatment room which is usually empty. I think all the gear we bought is stacked in there.'

'We bought'? He was indeed a generous boss if he'd actually spent money to set up a secure place for Maggie's baby. Or she was an assistant beyond price.

Sarah went in search of Jane who showed her the

small room already furnished not only with a cot but with sheets and a light blanket. Above the cot someone had hung a mobile of brightly coloured fish, and a variety of soft toys were lined up on the small pillow.

'I'm married and hoping to start a family but I want to keep working, part time at least, so Maggie and I decided to do this properly,' Jane explained. 'Once Adam agreed we commandeered this room. I don't know whether he's been in it since we began, but I dare say he won't object.'

She waved her hand towards the yellow gingham curtains which, when drawn, would cut out the sunshine, while still letting in some light. It was ideal.

'We pushed the treatment table over against the wall so you can use it as a changing table. The playpen's in the cupboard, and some other toys your Sam might like. Things Maggie and I couldn't resist when we were shopping.'

She opened the door to reveal an array of plastic toys in bright solid colours of red, blue, green and yellow. All looked sturdy as well as attractive, and Sam was already trying to wriggle out of her arms to get at a tempting ball.

'Later,' she told him. 'When you've had your sleep. You can sit in the playpen and throw it out as much as you like.'

He seemed to understand, snuggling into her shoulder and yawning obligingly.

'Is there a kitchen where I could heat some water?' she asked Jane, and was led to yet another small room with a table, bench, sink, refrigerator and microwave.

'Lunch-room,' Jane announced. 'Can I help?'

Sarah smiled at her. It was obvious from the interest in Jane's eyes that it hadn't been the question she'd wanted to ask, but at the moment the fewer people who knew of her complicated relationship to Adam the better.

'I'll manage,' she replied. 'I imagine you're busy enough with Maggie not here.'

Jane didn't exactly agree, but she did depart, leaving Sarah to find the formula she'd packed, a clean bottle and some boiled water she'd also brought from Adam's house. She mixed the milk then heated it in the microwave.

Sam tried to grab the bottle, but she held it until she had him in the redecorated room.

'There, you can have it while I change you,' she told him, smiling as the first mouthful produced a look of blissful contentment on his chubby face.

He was asleep before she put him in the cot, but she left the room reluctantly. It was a lovely room with bright things for his eyes to explore when he awoke, but would he panic in the strange place if she didn't hear his cries?

Adam came in as she headed uncertainly towards the door, his eyes widening at the sight of the 'renovations'.

'They did go to town, didn't they?' he said mildly, then, as he glanced down at the sleeping baby, he smiled. 'Jane said to tell you there's a monitor on the wall. The receiver is in the cupboard. Apparently you turn it on, stick it in your pocket and can then go anywhere within the complex. If he wakes you'll hear him cry, wherever you are.'

He spoke softly, telling her what she needed to know, but his attention was on the child. He moved closer, leaned across the cot, then reached out and brushed his fingers, with infinite gentleness, across the soft baby curls.

'Fiona had so much hair when she was born that she

looked like a little rag doll. People kept telling my mother she'd lose it, but I don't think she ever did.'

He straightened and glanced towards Sarah who had found the receiver and was waiting to leave the room.

'I was eight when she was born so I remember her like this,' he said, and the sadness in his voice told Sarah just how much he'd cared for his sister.

And how unwilling he might be to give up Fiona's child?

CHAPTER FIVE

SARAH didn't voice her doubts but walked with Adam back to the room where the testing devices were set up.

'Here are the cards.' He handed her a sheaf of cards the size of A4 paper, elaborately ruled to divide them into sections. 'You'll soon work out what goes where. We start by recording their fitness statistics at the top left, then each week we retest them and note down any changes.'

'Wouldn't it be more efficient, doing this on a computer?' Sarah asked, reading through the headings on the top card. 'Then you could call up different sections of the information and use the figures for comparisons and future research —a thousand things.'

He chuckled, as if he found her input amusing, and the sound of the soft ripple of laughter lingered in Sarah's head, distracting her as she tried to listen to his reply.

'That's one of Jane's duties—typing it all into the computer. I stick to the cards because individuals like to check their records. They get a kick out of seeing their condition improve. I could do a print-out each week, but the cards seem to work better. You watch—when this session ends most of those participating will wander casually over to where I leave the cards and leaf through them to find their own.'

It was Sarah's turn to chuckle as she pictured the scene.

'Do they check to see if they're as unfit as the measurements suggest or if we've documented their results correctly?'

'A bit of both, I guess. It's the beginning of an interest in their own level of fitness which some of them will retain for the rest of their lives,' he explained. 'Even though most of these kids have swum in school carnivals, perhaps even inter-school meets, few of them have got serious about their swimming. Now that there's an opportunity to travel to the World University Games in Vienna as an incentive, they're willing to give training a go.'

They'd traversed the gym and now paused at the far end. Sarah wanted to know more before they began work.

'But don't some of our top swimmers attend this university? Even far off in the west, I've heard of it and know their names. Won't they be the ones chosen to go?'

He studied her for a moment, then said, 'Do you always plunge right in to whatever you're doing, like this? Is that how you came to take on Fiona?'

She wanted to protest that Fiona had been a human problem, while this was professional, but there was something in his scrutiny which unnerved her and made her body feel uneasy. Before she could reply he was speaking again.

'Bad comparison! We'll talk about Fiona later. To answer your question, yes, the top swimmers will be chosen if they can spare the time from national commitments, but there are only a few of them, which leaves opportunities for any of this lot to make the squad. It's still twelve months until the meet, which means serious training won't begin until spring semester.'

'So these students could be well ahead of other hopefuls by then.'

Now he grinned at her, exacerbating the uneasiness riffling along her nerves.

'That's the idea,' he said, and led her into the room. 'OK, gang, let's get started. While I take you one at a time for physicals, you'll be working together, measuring body fat. To get a precise measurement, I should weigh you first on dry land and then in a pool—hydrostatic weighing—but as I don't have the pool or underwater scales we go on skin-fold tests. Pinch tests.'

The jokes began again but when Adam continued talking they stopped immediately. They might fool around, these young people, but when it came to getting fit they were serious.

For now!

'You'll measure the skin fold at four sites.' He pulled a student towards him to demonstrate. 'The subscapular, here under the shoulder-blade, abdomen, near your belly button, triceps and chest. Your partner will measure the amount of skin you've pinched and take an average of your four measurements, then Sarah will convert the measurement to an estimated percentage of body fat. Later on, we'll talk about what these percentages mean and what the optimum body fat is for you as swimmers. Now, sort yourself into pairs and get started. Jake, you come with me. I'll do your physical first.'

He sorted through the cards to find Jake's, showed Sarah where to find the callipers her charges would need and the chart for converting average skin-fold thickness to a body fat percentage, then disappeared through another door.

It was a hilarious half-hour, partners giggling as the pinching became personal and risque remarks shooting back and forth across the room. Jake returned and sent the next person, card in hand, in to Adam.

'He said to do weight next, then aerobic capacity. I've used the exercise machine before so I can hook them up for that if you like. I'll do my skin-fold later.'

'Great, I'll channel them your way when they're finished here,' she told him, and sent the first pair to him almost immediately.

She was recording the last weight—apart from Jake's—when the monitor alerted her to Sam's waking chortles. At least he wasn't distressed at waking in the strange room. Another victory for the good guys.

'I'll leave the cards here so you can write in your aerobic capacity when Jake's done with you,' she told the group. 'And take your card when you go in to see the doctor.'

She hurried away, surprised by how much she'd enjoyed the interaction with the group. Was it this particular group—or the fact that she'd had so little contact with people for the past year?

Sam was standing in the cot, rattling at the railing and laughing at the antics of a clown doll manipulated by Adam.

'Aren't you supposed to be doing physicals?' Sarah snapped, disconcerted by, but unable to control, a fierce surge of—fear? No, she didn't think Adam would harm the baby. Not jealousy, surely? She couldn't be jealous of Sam's acceptance of the man.

'The students can spare me a five-minute break. I heard him wake—my surgery's right next to this room—so I thought I'd better assure him that rescue was at hand. I didn't go so far as to pick him up.'

Sarah sniffed the air. 'Bet I can guess why,' she sniped, then she turned to smile at Sam.

'Had a good sleep, darling?'

He held out his arms to her and blew a raspberry of delight. The reaction reassured her of his love and settled some of the butterflies, fidgeting in her stomach. She was beginning to suspect the others would remain a-flutter whenever she was close to Adam Fletcher—and not entirely because of her uncertainty over Sam.

'He's due for lunch. I've finished recording the weight and body-fat measurements and Jake's handling the aerobic capacity. Is there anything else you need me to do right now?'

He studied her for a moment, before answering. 'Look, I didn't ask you to work here to make a slave of you. I thought it would give us more time to get—oh, I don't know—a feel for each other, I guess.'

He grinned, cast his eyes towards the ceiling and muttered, 'And that didn't come out right either. Change the child and feed him. By then I should be through and we can sit down in my office and have a chat.'

He headed purposefully out of the door.

'A feel for each other, indeed,' Sarah said to Sam, who also grinned.

He was clean, fed and happily exploring the waiting room, by pushing the ball into barely accessible places then crawling in to retrieve it, by the time Adam reappeared. Jane was explaining the basics of the computer system to Sarah so the first she knew of his arrival was Sam's shout of welcome.

'I'll put the playpen in my office—you get some toys. Sam can play in it while we talk.'

Sarah followed him out of the room, feeling no happier about the coming interview than he had sounded. Sam was sitting on the ball, balancing himself by holding onto a chair leg, and smiling delightedly at Jane who was clapping at his trick.

I'm putting myself through all this turmoil for you, she told him silently. He waved to her when he saw her and promptly toppled off his perch.

'Leave him here—he's no bother,' Jane said, but the words were barely out of her mouth when the doors slid open and two men entered the room, the larger one clutching at his shoulder, his face grey with pain.

'Is Adam in?' the other demanded. 'Can he take a look at Richard? He fell awkwardly when we were stacking the practice gear away and put his hand out to save himself. I thought it was a shoulder dislocation but couldn't feel the head of the humerus to try to get it back in place.'

'Come through to the X-ray room. I'll call Adam,' Jane said, leading them down the hall.

X-ray room? Sarah wondered just what else Adam had tucked away in this building. Most doctors sent their patients to specialist radiography centres for X-rays. She was still wondering about it when Jane returned.

'He'll need strapping. Adam said could you get out some one-and-a-half-inch tape and a shoulder sling? He said you'd find it on the top shelf labelled "Acromio-clavicular Harness".'

Did he need her as a nurse or was he simply keeping an eye on her? Couldn't Jane assist him? Would he need professional help?

'Off you go. I'll keep an eye on Sam,' Jane said, so Sarah made her way back to the small treatment room, her uneasiness growing and with it her aggravation with the man who was causing it.

She found the awkward-looking harness and had the tape and scissors ready by the time Adam returned with the patient. The man who had accompanied him must have been waiting outside.

'The X-ray shows a shoulder separation,' Adam explained after a brief introduction which consisted of him saying tersely, 'Richard, Sarah. Sarah, Richard.'

'The ligaments of the joint are torn, which pushes the head of the clavicle out of alignment. Strapping helps to keep it in place while the ligaments heal. Strapping and rest—six to eight weeks' rest.'

He spoke the last words to the patient, his face stern and his voice severe.

'I mean it, Richard. No football, no training that involves your arm or shoulder. If you don't let the ligaments heal you'll end up needing surgery to repair them, and that will put you out of action for up to six months with a likelihood of bad arthritic problems later in your life.'

'But you said Grade Two, Fletch—that's not the worst,' the burly man objected. 'Surely, with some strapping and extra padding when I play...'

'Six weeks minimum,' Adam said emphatically, 'and I'll X-ray it again before I give an all-clear. Now, stop arguing with me and let me get you strapped. Sarah, could you wipe his shoulder down with alcohol then get a couple of squares of felt from the box where you found the harness? One goes on his shoulder and the other under his elbow. The idea is to provide downward pressure on the clavicle and upward forearm pressure from below the elbow.'

Was he telling the patient this or her? Did he think she needed to know or did he sense her interest?

Whatever the reason, he talked as he strapped, instructing her what lengths of tape he wanted and explaining why he set it where he did, overlapping it to give the joint support.

Richard also talked. It was polite conversation, nothing more, although Adam's attitude made it seem less casual, particularly when it turned from general to personal and focussed on Sarah.

'You're new here?' Richard asked, and Adam forestalled her reply.

'Maggie had her baby this morning. Sarah's filling in on a temporary basis.'

Perhaps! Sarah felt like saying. Maybe! Depending on your attitude.

'Done much fitness work?' Richard asked.

'None at all,' Sarah admitted.

'It's a holiday job for her,' Adam cut in, putting out his hand for another strip of tape.

'Been on the coast long?' Not a man to give in easily, this Richard!

'Arrived yesterday.'

'I could show you around,' Richard offered. 'Now I've been banged up like this, and Hitler here insists I rest the shoulder, I won't be doing much.'

'I'll be showing her around,' Adam said, before Sarah could formulate a polite refusal.

'Well, perhaps a drink one night?' Richard persisted, and Sarah, puzzled by his interest, looked at him more closely and saw him wink at her. He was assuming that she and Adam were involved and was setting Adam up—teasing him.

She returned his wink and smiled sweetly.

'That might be fun,' she said, then winced as the next piece of tape was snatched from her fingers.

'Aren't you forgetting Sam?' Adam demanded, and when Richard looked puzzled he added, 'Her baby!'

Sarah stiffened. This man was beginning to irritate her. Richard had been right with his Hitler crack! How dared he decide what she did and with whom she did it? Not that she wanted to go out with Richard. In fact, she didn't want a social life with anyone at the moment. Her relationship with Sam was still too tenuous to be jeopardised. But surely the right of refusal should be hers.

'Perhaps you could babysit him,' she said sweetly. 'After all, it was your idea for Sam and I to stay on for a while.'

Richard chuckled. 'I think she's got you there, old mate,' he said. 'And what's with you, anyway? What's happened to your sense of humour? You can usually smell a set-up before I've even figured out how I'll do it.'

He turned his attention back to Sarah.

'We went to school together,' he explained. 'In fact, he was a better footballer than I am, but he decided to use his brains to make his money while I decided brawn might offer more.'

'In the short term it probably did,' Adam pointed out, 'but once you start collecting injuries like this you should be thinking seriously of retirement.'

'Oh, I am! Thirty-four's too old for the game. In fact, I'd intended making this my last season even before this happened. I've been offered a job as a commentator and someone's asked me to do a book.'

He smiled at Sarah.

'Does that make me sound more eligible than a foot-baller?'

'For some woman, maybe,' she agreed.

'But not for you?' he asked, glancing from her to Adam as if puzzled by her presence in his friend's life.

'No, not for me,' she said. 'Sam's the only male I want in my life at the moment.'

She saw Adam glance up from what he was doing, frowning at her as if questioning this assertion. She handed him another strip of tape and this time he took it gently, his fingers brushing hers. A silent apology for his earlier behaviour? Or was she imagining things?

Whatever it was, it ended the silly conversation.

'Now,' he said, when strips were in place across Richard's shoulder and down under his forearm, 'in the old days we then strapped the arm to the patient's chest, which meant untold agony for hairy folk like Richard when we removed the strips and ripped off hair and sometimes skin.'

He hesitated, as if considering the tape. 'Perhaps...'

'Don't you dare!' Richard warned him. 'I've told you I was only teasing. Though why you got uppity I don't know. Sarah's not your type.' He grinned at Sarah. 'Dark beauties are more his line. Right from when he was at school it was the brunettes he went for. Suited me as I always fancied blondes myself so we didn't have to argue over it.'

'I think I will use the tape—perhaps across your mouth.'

Richard raised his uninjured arm.

'Pax!' he pleaded. 'Not the tape!'

Sarah watched the interaction between the two men, sensing their fondness for each other beneath the light-hearted teasing. She found herself wishing she had a friend like that—someone who understood her well enough to tease her. Growing up in the country and doing her schooling by correspondence, she'd missed out on making childhood friends.

There'd been the kids she'd mucked about with during

holidays at the beach, others at the surf-club and fellow competitors in teenage surfing events, but she'd always had to go back home when summer had ended, leaving them in their tight-knit groups.

Then— No, she wouldn't think about Colin.

She'd become friendly with fellow students during her nursing study and training, but they'd drifted apart when work had separated them.

Sam would grow up with friends, she promised herself fiercely. If she did nothing else right in his life, she'd make sure of that!

'I suppose I'll take pity on you and use the harness to hold it all together.' Adam's words recalled her to the job in hand and she watched as he positioned it. 'It also helps apply the downward pressure and keeps the fore-arm in position to push upward, and can be adjusted to fit any patient.'

He slipped the harness over the taped area and indicated to Sarah to hold it while he tightened the straps, motioning for her to come closer.

She'd been better off when she'd been thinking about relationships, she realised. Now she was standing wedged between the two men, yet only one of them set her senses tingling with an alertness that made her want to shiver. Richard was obviously a superbly fit athlete, his chest well muscled without being overly large, so why could she treat him with the dispassionate compo-sure she felt for any patient yet react to every accidental touch of skin on skin from Adam? Particularly as she had it on good authority that she wasn't his type!

It couldn't be because she knew him better—she knew nothing of the man apart from his ability to organise things his way.

'This buckle!' he said sharply, and she grasped her

wandering wits and with clumsy fingers fumbled at the fastening he was indicating. 'Now I'll pull the strap to tighten it,' he added. 'Yell if it hurts,' he told Richard.

Sarah stepped away, wanting to escape—to get away from the room, the man and the unwelcome answers to her own questions.

Sam was back in the cot and sound asleep by the time she reached the waiting room.

'He was yawning and rubbing his eyes so I changed him and dumped him into bed,' Jane explained, after she'd shown Richard out and filed his card. She studied Sarah for a few seconds then added, 'For someone filling in out of the goodness of her heart, Adam's working you fairly hard, isn't he?'

It was a mild probe, considering the curiosity that must be churning through Jane's mind! As things stood, it would have to remain unsatisfied.

'I don't know how hard he usually works his nurse,' Sarah replied. 'Thanks for taking care of Sam. I don't think I'll be doing Maggie's job full time. You shouldn't have to be responsible for him when you've your own work to do.'

'Jane won't have to keep an eye on him.'

Adam did his materialising act again, appearing so quietly both women spun to face him.

'He swears he doesn't creep up on us deliberately, that he's just naturally soft-footed, but he scares the living daylights out of me and Maggie about ten times a day.'

Soft-footed? Such a big man? Sarah watched him move closer and realised she'd spoke the truth. Big as he was, he walked with an athlete's grace, so perfectly balanced that his feet seemed to brush across the floor.

Jane demanded an explanation of his words, but it was to Sarah he explained.

'I spoke to Jacinta, one of the swimmers. She's doing a thesis this year for her MA so doesn't attend lectures, and she's worked her way through university, babysitting. I have several friends who use her regularly who'd be pleased to give you references, and I know she'd be glad to earn some extra money, taking care of Sam.'

'I— She—' About to add a 'he' to the lame beginnings, Sarah shut her mouth. What she wanted to say was stop rushing me. And stop organising my life. And Sam's! But unless she could think of a valid objection any protest would sound petty, not to mention feeding Jane's curiosity. She threw him a dirty look so he wouldn't think he was getting away with this behaviour and resolved to argue it out with him later.

He was singularly unaffected by the dirty look, merely smiling as her words stumbled to a halt then saying, 'So, with that settled, how about we leave Jane to get on with her work while you come into my office and we'll talk about your duties?'

'I can imagine which of "we" will do the talking,' Sarah muttered as she followed him along the corridor.

They passed the second treatment room and she looked in on Sam, who was lying on his back with his arms outflung, so beautiful her heart clenched with the love she felt for him.

OK, Adam Fletcher, you win this round. I'll do more than listen to your list of duties for the sake of that child.

It was a concession which should have made her feel better, but as she walked into his office her chest grew tight with apprehension and her body stiffened in preparation for whatever battle lay ahead.

'As I said earlier, you don't have to work here,' he began. 'Talking about your duties got us away from Jane, without too many questions being asked.'

He smiled at her, breaching her defences so easily that the direction of her annoyance switched from him to herself.

'You've seen today a little of the type of work you'd do. I can get Jacinta to mind Sam, and working together would give us time to get to know each other. To me, it seems sensible but...' He lifted one shoulder in a questioning kind of shrug and the movement drew Sarah's attention to his body and diverted her into thinking of him as a footballer...

'If you'd prefer to stay on at the house but not work, we'd still have time to talk at evenings and weekends. I've had temps work here with me before, so there are no problems there.'

She set aside the image of him in football shorts and concentrated on the live being.

'You're being very obliging all of a sudden,' she said, eyeing him warily. 'Quite a change from the man who's been barking orders at me since we first met.'

Dark eyebrows climbed towards his hairline.

'Me? Barking orders at you?'

He sounded so incredulous that she smiled, but it was time to take a stand before this man totally took over her life.

'Come here, go there, do this, do that—if you're not barking orders you're making arrangements without the slightest consideration of how I might feel.'

'You don't want Jacinta minding Sam—is that the problem? Would you rather find someone else? Mind him yourself?'

Sarah studied him closely. Was he genuinely put out or teasing her? Not knowing made her edgy.

'Since I've met Jacinta and she has experience, I guess it's OK,' she conceded. 'It's just that you take all this on yourself. I'm not even sure I want to work here and already you've organised a babysitter!' It was her turn to shrug. 'I guess I'm not used to people telling me what to do.'

His smile came and went so quickly she wondered if she'd imagined it.

'Fiona used to tell me to stop organising her,' Adam said softly. 'I didn't know I did it until she yelled at me about it one day.'

Sarah heard regret and love and pain all mixed up in his voice and she forgot her objections to his manner, wanting only to offer comfort to him.

'We had the same arguments, Fiona and I,' she admitted. 'I tried to help her, without seeming to take over her life, but—'

'It's near impossible,' Adam finished for her, when it seemed she'd forgotten what she'd wanted to say—or had wandered so far back into her thoughts she'd lost her way.

He studied her, intrigued by this woman who had catapulted herself into his life, but he shouldn't be intrigued—he had to be wary. Too much was at stake for him to forget his suspicions and doubts.

'Why don't we take each day as it comes?' he suggested, hoping he sounded more businesslike than he felt. 'Think about it this afternoon, and if you want to come to work with me tomorrow I'll organise Jacinta.'

The suggestion, which had seemed eminently sensible to him, didn't meet with her approval, judging from the frown she turned on him.

'There's something wrong with the idea?' he asked, then hoped it hadn't sounded like a demand.

'No, not really,' Sarah said slowly, as though taking each day as it came was a new concept for her. 'But if we're working together I don't see the necessity for me to live in your house. Sam and I can move to a hotel or get a small unit somewhere. This is a holiday destination so there'd be short-term rental units available.'

Definitely not the time to forget suspicions!

'Why would you want to do that when I've plenty of room in a perfectly adequate house?' This time he didn't care if it did sound like a demand.

'Because you don't trust me,' she retorted. 'You've made it perfectly obvious and I can't say I blame you. So why would you want me living in your house? What if you're called out? Are you going to be happy to leave me there, feeling as you do?'

He noticed again the sparks that flashed in her eyes when she was angry, and wondered if other emotions— No, he wouldn't wonder about that right now. There was lost ground he had to retrieve.

'I didn't say I didn't trust you,' he argued, 'just that I wouldn't sign Sam over to someone I didn't know.' He hoped he sounded more convincing than he felt because right now he wasn't quite certain why he wanted her to stay. 'That's why I suggested you work here.'

'You suggested I work here because Maggie had her baby early and I was on the spot. It was convenience.'

Yes, the sparks were still there, but he fancied they were less fiery—as if she was arguing for the sake of it. Not that he minded an argument...

'Only partly,' he agreed, deciding it was time to get the conversation back on track. 'Will you at least think it over?'

It made sense, Sarah knew, and the house would provide some temporary stability for Sam. Why was she hesitating?

'I don't want to be dependent on you,' she objected.

'If I stay I can look after myself. Once I've done some shopping I can fix meals for myself and Sam.' She wasn't quite agreeing, but coming close. 'Particularly for Sam. He's lived on tinned and bottled food for long enough. In fact, I should shop today. I'm also running short of disposable nappies.'

She was blathering again—talking so fast the words tripped over each other—but his smile was making her heart jiggle about in her chest. It was so blatantly triumphant she knew he guessed she'd given in and considered this round his. The smile should have made her angry, not started her organs jiggling.

'Then let's go while the child is sleeping,' he said. 'There's a shopping centre just down the road—walking distance. We can be back in half an hour.'

'Let's go as in let *us* go?' she queried, panicked by the domesticity of shopping with the man, given the unreliability of her reactions to him. 'I can manage on my own.'

'Ah, but I need some lunch. I'm sure you do, too. We can grab a sandwich or whatever while we're out and bring it back. I'll be your guide.'

She hesitated, wanting to argue—to protest about him coming—but there was no valid reason she could give to refuse what was, to him, a simple kindness. She could hardly tell him he unsettled her—that she needed time away from him—when they barely knew each other.

'I thought you wanted to talk,' she muttered, grasping at a straw that might delay this expedition.

'Can't you talk and walk?' he teased.

Having him tease her wasn't much fun either! That glint in his eyes was as dangerous as his smile.

CHAPTER SIX

THEY walked and talked and shopped. The experience was quite unnerving, Adam decided. So much so he regretted he'd suggested it.

For a start, choosing fruit and vegetables with a woman by his side, or watching her make her selections, was surprisingly pleasant, and that fact alone disconcerted him. Not that he meant to do it on a permanent basis. No, he'd decided long ago that getting too close to people led to pain—Fiona being the prime example.

While it was mildly amusing to watch his house-guest tease at her lip with the tip of her tongue as she debated the virtue of pumpkin over carrots, he didn't think he should be enjoying it.

'Is it so vital—what vegetables he eats?' he asked, beguiled by Sarah's fastidious approach and wanting to divert his mind from his reaction to the situation.

She spun, as if his voice had startled her. Had she forgotten he was with her? Would another woman have discounted him so readily? So much for diversions!

'I don't suppose so,' she muttered, putting both pumpkin and carrots into the shopping trolley he was holding and moving determinedly towards the next aisle. 'I'm sorry if I'm holding you up. I'm not used to shopping with someone else—except Sam, of course.'

More intrigue!

'Do you always take him everywhere with you? Is there no one who would mind him?' He considered how his mother always seized the opportunity to mind small children, proclaiming under-fives were far more interesting than adults. 'Your mother? Other family?'

She stopped and he cannoned into her, the trolley hitting her firmly in the back.

'I have no family,' she said, then she strode on again, leaving him to follow with even more questions jangling in his brain.

Was this a ploy to make him feel sorry for her? If it was true, would it explain her determination to keep someone else's baby? If he accepted that one fact, would he then have to accept everything else? And, damn it all, why didn't she have a family? Everyone had a family.

He studied her as she pulled bulky packs of disposable nappies from the shelf, almost filling the trolley with their mass. Was she, in spite of her healthy appearance, another Fiona? Had she lost her family in the pursuit of the oblivion of drugs?

No, that didn't fit. She might be pale, but her skin had the gleam only good health brought and her muscles were too well developed for anyone who'd given up on exercise, particularly in her legs. And looking at her legs as she reached up to the shelf wasn't the most brilliant move he'd made all day! He shook his head.

'I'm sorry, but he does need a lot. At home I use cloth nappies, but travelling…'

Her voice trailed away and he looked up to find her watching him warily. It took him a moment to realise she was responding to his head shake—and that she'd caught him, looking at her legs.

'Get as many as you need,' he assured her, steeling himself against an urge to sneak another glance downward to check if they really were as exquisitely shapely as they'd seemed.

She didn't reply but moved along the aisle, adding a tin of formula to the other items then heading towards the meat display. Perhaps it was time to take a stand.

'Look, you're staying in my house as my guest. Tell me what you like eating and I'll look after it.'

The glance she threw his way was one of pure scorn.

'Do you have a freezer? Can I get enough meat for a few days?'

'I've got meat in the freezer,' he protested, aware he was losing ground fast. 'It would be ridiculous, the two of us cooking separate meals in the same kitchen.'

'Then I'll cook for you while I'm visiting. It would be one way of paying our board.'

Her eyes met his and he read the challenge there. If he kept arguing, would she refuse to stay with him?

To his surprise, he found himself capitulating.

'OK, you cook,' he said quickly, anxious to divert her from voicing the hotel option again.

Another win for me or another knot, tying me to this man I'd prefer never to have met? Sarah threw some packs of chicken breasts on top of the other shopping, found eggs and added them, then turned up another aisle to find her favourite breakfast cereal.

Perhaps it's the thought of sharing living space with an adult, she comforted herself, but she knew it wasn't true. If Adam hadn't startled her hormones back to reluctant life she'd have happily shared his house while he checked her out.

And speaking of check-outs...

She led the way towards the exits, anticipating their next confrontation. Instinct told her this man wouldn't stand by while a woman paid—even for her own necessities—so no doubt they'd have a ding-dong battle in front of the cashier.

'I'll pay,' he announced, parking the trolley against the counter and moving ahead of her to smile winsomely at the young woman behind the till.

'You will do no such thing,' Sarah countered, trying vainly to distract the woman's attention from Adam. 'This is almost all baby stuff, and he's my baby so I'll pay!'

'If what you say's correct, he's mine too,' Adam countered, turning to her with a grin of mischievous delight. The check-out operator looked from Adam to Sarah then turned back to Adam again. It was obvious what she thought and who she'd back in an argument.

'As one of us will undoubtedly pay, you may start putting the items through,' Sarah told her tartly.

The young woman started visibly then remembered her job and began to run the selection one by one across the scanner, contenting herself with casting occasional black looks at Sarah and small prim smiles in Adam's direction.

He must have caught them because he was looking unbearably smug—enough to make Sarah wish she had control of the trolley and could run over his foot.

The bill was totalled and, ignoring Sarah completely, the woman turned to Adam and announced the amount. Determined not to give her the pleasure of hearing the fight she intended having with this man the moment they were outside the store, Sarah gritted her teeth and watched as he reached into his hip pocket.

And pulled out his hand—empty!

She felt her smile begin to twitch at the corner of her lips but held it in check. He patted his other pockets then slid his fingers into the back one again. Sarah tipped her head back and gazed at the ceiling, trying for a look of long-suffering patience.

'I haven't brought my wallet,' he mumbled at her. 'I'm always telling other men not to leave their wallets in their hip pockets as the bulk affects the way they sit— pushes their pelvis out of alignment—so I got into the habit of taking it out and putting it in my drawer when I got to work...'

The check-out operator had the grace to look embarrassed as she turned hopefully to Sarah, but she wasn't going to let Adam off that easily.

'Then how are you going to pay?' she asked him. 'I don't think they have dishes you can wash.'

She didn't hear the noise but she could have sworn he ground his teeth at her in reply. Pulling her wallet slowly and carefully out of the carry-all, she extracted the necessary notes and change and handed them over.

He was out of the supermarket, pushing the trolley at racing speed across the food court of the shopping centre, before she caught up with him.

'Now, what did you want for lunch? My shout.'

He stopped abruptly, then turned slowly, shaking his head as he looked down into her face.

'Are you sure you haven't got the wrong man? Isn't there anyone else you could cast in the role of Sam's uncle?'

The questions were so unexpected she stared at him blankly. She'd been thinking lunch, but what had he been pondering?

Then he smiled and added, 'I suppose it's my own fault for insisting you stay. I'll have a salad roll. The shop over there by the chemist makes beauties.'

He nodded towards a sandwich bar then slumped onto a convenient seat, settled his forearms on the trolley and rested his head on top of them, looking for all the world like a man who'd conceded defeat.

Sam was still sleeping when they returned to the clinic. Not wanting to eat with Adam in the small room Jane had called the lunch-room, Sarah offered to eat her sandwich at the reception desk to relieve Jane while she had her lunch.

'There shouldn't be any problems,' Jane told her. 'Roger Smythe is coming in at three—he'll be the next. His card is already out on the counter so if he comes in early check that Fletch is ready to see him then show him in.'

When she'd departed Sarah picked up the card, interested in the type of 'patients' Adam—Fletch—saw. The unusual surname also rang a bell, and when she read about the current injury, plantar fasciitis, she realised why. He was a runner, recently in the news for turning from sprinting to middle-distance running. Leafing through his past injuries, Sarah wondered why anyone pursued sport so relentlessly.

According to the notes, he'd been treated for pulled calf and thigh muscles, shin splints, tendonitis in both knees—fortunately, at different times—and some mysterious problem connected with a tight iliotibial band, for which the doctor had prescribed specific stretching exercises.

Fascinated by the details of this, to her, new branch of medicine, she turned back to the first entry and began to read both the patient's description of his problems and the doctor's comments.

'I'm Roger Smythe. I've an appointment.'

Sarah looked up guiltily, then reminded herself that working here gave her the right of access to patient files.

'I'm Sarah,' she told the slight, lean, bony man who leaned against the reception counter. 'I'll just see if Dr Fletcher's free.'

As she headed for his office she heard the patient repeat her formal 'Dr Fletcher' in amused tones.

'Your patient's here,' she said, poking her head around the door after first tapping and being told to enter. 'Shall I send him in?'

'Patient?' Adam looked up from what was evidently some of his 'paperwork' and frowned at her.

'Roger Smythe.' Sarah moved into the room and handed him the card, but before he read it Adam's face cleared.

'Having trouble with his plantar fascia—do you know what that is?'

Pleased she'd read the notes, Sarah responded, 'It's fibrous connective tissue in the foot which is stretched by the weight of the body during running.'

'Did you read the notes or, like an open Gibney, was it something you've experienced or learnt about?'

'I read the notes,' Sarah admitted, regretting her action when she saw him smile. 'Shall I send the man in?'

The smile grew wider when he heard the aggravation in her voice. 'If you would be so kind, Miss Tremayne,' he replied in dulcet tones. Then he added, 'And if Sam's still sleeping, and Jane's finished lunch, come in yourself. I want to try some arch supports. Are you any good at whittling?'

He waved his hand, dismissing her before she could demand an explanation of such a weird question. Jane was back behind the reception desk and Sam was still catching up on missed sleep so she accompanied Roger into the doctor's room.

'Have you been following orders?' Adam asked, and Roger saluted, an action Sarah felt she'd be likely to use herself in the not-too-distant future.

'Resting, soaking it in warm water, doing non-weight-bearing exercise—which is a bore—then using ice,' he said. 'I can pick up marbles with my toes better than any monkey and I've been strapping it in between exercising.' He paused, then added, 'I suppose it's some indication of improvement that I've been taking less aspirin to control the pain.'

'Let's have a look,' Adam suggested. When the patient took off his shoe and stripped off his sock she saw the strapping across the sole of his foot.

Adam removed it, then prodded and pressed, eliciting soft reactive gasps from Roger when he touched the tender spots.

'I'm going to try you with a standard support, but if it doesn't fit correctly you may need to have one made up,' he said, straightening from his examination and picking up a hard plastic prosthetic device from his desk. 'Slip this in your shoe and stand up.'

Sarah waited, still wondering where whittling came into it

'Hurts like hell!' Roger complained when he put his weight on the foot.

'Thought it might,' Adam responded, motioning for his patient to sit. 'You've always been too flat-footed to make a decent runner.'

Expecting a protest from this man, who'd won medals at Olympic events, Sarah was surprised to hear him laugh. He must have sensed her bewilderment for he said easily, 'It's an old argument we have. In fact, he's the one with foot trouble—puts his in his mouth more often than not.'

Once again Sarah was struck by the relaxed conversation between patient and doctor, the relationship between the pair seeming more like friendship.

'I use this sponge and first shape it to approximately

the same shape as the rigid device, then I whittle it down until it feels comfortable to Roger.'

'Isn't that a subjective judgement?' she asked, interest drawing her into the conversation.

'Yes, but it's also just the beginning.' Adam whittled at the inflexible foam, cutting away until the shape was more or less the same as the device. He then tried it in the shoe, making Roger stand and concentrate on where it hurt.

With the foam in his hands again, he cut away at the points where it had produced pressure, trying it again and again until his patient finally bore his weight entirely on that foot without flinching.

'Now it's your turn,' Adam announced, passing the foam to Sarah. 'Cut a quarter of an inch from the bottom while I soften some Plasticine.'

Too bemused to argue, she cut into the foam, surprised to find the job less difficult than she'd expected. Handing it back to Adam, she watched as he spread a pad of Plasticine across the shaped side, then once again asked Roger to bear his weight on it.

'I give the impression to a plastics manufacturer,' Adam belatedly explained. 'He'll make a rigid device that hopefully will be exactly what Roger needs to support the foot while it heals.'

'Why don't you use the foam?' Sarah asked, thinking of how firm it had felt in her hands.

'It compacts in time and would then do more harm than good,' Adam told her, but he smiled—the nice smile which made her heart jiggle, not the sardonic one which prompted thoughts of physical violence! She had the silly idea that he was pleased by her interest in his work.

Though why he should be...

When Roger left, Adam showed her sketches of feet, explaining what happened when the tissues were injured.

'Some athletes have problems with tightness in their plantar fascia,' he added. 'We have a very scientific exercise for that.' Reaching into a cupboard behind him, he withdrew a small glass Coca-Cola bottle. 'A foot fits neatly into this waisted part so the patient can roll it under his sole to stretch the tissues.'

'Did you learn about the Coke bottle in your studies?' Sarah asked, and won another smile.

'Sports medicine is a relatively new field. There have always been medical specialists who've had interests in particular sports—for instance, orthopaedic specialists who concentrate on football injuries, and top-line sportsmen and -women have had various consultants. My work encompasses a wider spread of patients. I treat some of Australia's top swimmers because they're based here on the Gold Coast, but I also give talks to the under-nine soccer team in the neighbouring suburb because I believe it's never too young to start people thinking about their fitness for sport.'

'Fitness for sport,' Sarah repeated. 'Don't people usually put it the other way around—sport for fitness?'

The smile became a chuckle, a warm, almost conspiratorial sound.

'I'm pleased you see the difference,' he said. 'An enormous number of injuries occur because people decide to get fit so they take up some form of sport or exercise, without realising their body needs a bit of preparation.'

She was about to ask about the preparation when the receiver she was carrying in her pocket alerted her to Sam's cries.

'Maybe having Jacinta here is a good idea,' she conceded, leaving the room—and their conversation—reluctantly.

'This is a very interesting place,' she told Sam as she lifted him from the cot. 'We could learn a lot here, you and I.'

Was her new-found fascination with sports medicine an excuse to give in to the man's demands and stay? But she had to stay, anyway, so why did she need an excuse?

She changed the baby and was carrying him back into the reception area when Adam appeared.

'If we leave now, Sam can have a play on the beach before his dinner,' he suggested.

Sarah stared at him, thinking of another problem that was certain to arise if she stayed on—mobility. Getting around without him chauffeuring them everywhere they went. It tied her too closely to his timetable—and to him.

'Are you ready to leave? Isn't there work you should be doing?'

'Worried my practice might go downhill if I leave early one afternoon, Miss Tremayne?'

This time his smile taunted her, reminding her of the distrust that lay beneath the surface charm he seemed able to turn on and off at will. She met the smile and matched it with one of her own which was just as false.

'Of course not,' she said.

His suspicion had wrecked the fragile rapport which had begun to grow between them as they'd worked. It manifested itself in uneasiness on the drive home, strengthening until Sarah decided she had to do something about it.

'Look,' she said, when they entered the big rumpus room on the lowest level of the house, she carrying Sam while Adam laboured under the assortment of plastic shopping bags, 'I can understand you being suspicious of a stranger landing on your doorstep so suddenly. Perhaps, before this goes any further—and before Sam explores your beach—you should have a look at my references. I'm not here after your money. I'm here after your signature.'

She thrust her hand into her carry-all and fished around for the leather folder where she kept her papers.

'Even the archbishop gave me a reference,' she told him, her fingers pushing aside bottles and jars, washcloths and her wallet, searching in the jumble for the feel of the soft leather.

Adam watched her, setting the bulging plastic bags on the floor and leaning against the wall beside the lift, his arms folded in an attitude that suggested he had all day to wait.

'Not there?' he said softly, his eyes dancing with delight as she faced the same dilemma he had earlier. 'Welcome to the club.'

She ignored his teasing, frowning as she tried to remember when she'd last seen the folder.

'Maybe I took it out and put it in the suitcase,' she muttered to herself.

'Are the references so important?'

Sarah stared at him.

'I would have thought you could answer that,' she said. 'Surely you wouldn't sign away a child without any idea about the person taking him?'

His eyes lost their gleam of humour, becoming darkly serious.

'My point exactly, Miss Tremayne, yet you expected me to do just that yesterday afternoon.'

'I expected you to check my references first,' she argued heatedly. 'And Sam's birth certificate, and the letter from the hospital, releasing him and Fiona to my care. I had—have—all of those somewhere. Any normal man would have looked at them yesterday—'

'Before you lost them?'

'You don't believe me!' Sarah felt despair settle on her shoulders.

'I don't disbelieve you,' he said calmly. 'Now, let's get this gear packed away and go down to the beach before it's too cold for the baby.'

'You don't have to come to the beach,' Sarah muttered, following him into the lift and trying to stand as far away from him as the packages allowed.

'No, but I usually have a swim when I get home so if you don't object to my presence on the same strip of sand...'

Now *she* felt like grinding her teeth. She'd met him a bare twenty-four hours earlier but already he knew precisely how to get under her skin.

The lift stopped at the first floor.

'This is my stop,' he said. 'I'll pack away the groceries, then bring up the baby stuff and leave it in your bedroom. You go on down to the beach.'

He was ordering her around again but Sarah bit back her protest. Sam had been cooped up inside all day—he needed some fresh air. So did she, for that matter, preferably air untainted by Adam Fletcher's presence.

Down at the beach she built sandcastles for Sam to knock over, enjoying the rough texture of the sand between her fingers and the salt tang to the air. A sense of well-being returned—but not for long.

'I'll leave my towel here,' a now-familiar voice said. Sarah glanced up from her architectural masterpiece, seeing first strong, suntanned calves, then thighs and finally an almost bare but beautifully formed body. The muscles were delineated beneath the skin, and there was no sign of excess body fat.

He'd walked on before she'd gathered sufficient wits to speak. Now she watched him stride through the shallow water then dive neatly into a curling wave, surfacing beyond the breakers and striking out to deeper water with clean, strong strokes.

Sam claimed her attention, and when she looked again Adam was riding a wave back towards the beach, his body arrowing towards the sand. Further out, a group of young men on surfboards called to each other, pointing out a set of breakers heading towards them.

As they paddled furiously to catch the first wave of the set, Sarah felt a surge of longing, remembering the frantic pull of arms through the water, then the uplift as the board caught the wave. Standing up, arms balancing the body, feet guiding the board—the exhilarating sense of flying through the air as you rushed towards the beach.

'You did some surfing?'

Again his voice surprised her, and she turned her attention from the surfers to find him bending to pick up his towel. Had that been his swim? Couldn't he have stayed away longer? Kept his water-glistened body out of her line of sight for a while?

'You weren't long,' she said aggrievedly, refusing to answer his question while he seemed bent on unsettling her body with his closeness.

'Got something in my eye,' he said. 'Perhaps a grain of sand. I rode the wave in too far up the beach.'

He sat on his towel, keeping away from Sam who was eyeing him warily as if uncertain whether this near-naked man was the same fellow he'd been smiling at earlier in the day.

'Is it out? Do you want me to take a look?' The practical nurse said the words automatically, horrifying the emotional part of Sarah who knew that getting physically closer to this man—for any reason—was not a good idea.

He blinked before he answered, then grimaced.

'Yes, it's still there. Do you mind?'

'Of course not,' the nurse replied, while the other Sarah groaned inwardly.

Finding a clean handkerchief in her bag, she twirled one corner of it to a sharp point then moved so she could kneel in front of Adam. His body was so close she could see the droplets of water making their erratic way through the softly curling dark hairs on his chest.

'This eye?'' she asked, all business, although the errant part of her was distracted now by the thickness of his lashes.

'Yes, down low and towards the corner.'

She was close enough to feel his breath on her cheek, another diversion for the inner Sarah.

With gentle fingers she slid his lower lid downwards, catching sight of the speck of sand lodged against the eyeball.

'I should be able to ease it off,' she said, finding the words hard to form as her mouth unaccountably dried up. 'That's it. It will probably still feel sore if it's slightly scratched, but you'd know...'

Babbling again!

She sat back on her heels, but not quickly enough because he caught her wrist as she moved away, preventing total escape.

'Thanks!' he said, but his eyes weren't echoing the message. They were looking at her in a most peculiar

way, as if trying to understand a riddle or solve a puzzle
of some kind.

He'd been all right until she'd knelt beside him, Adam
realised. OK, so he'd been surprised by the lush figure
when he'd first spied her in the bathing suit, had even
felt a stirring which he'd put down to a purely masculine
reflex. But at the view of the top of creamy breasts bared
above the swimsuit, the close-up, one-eyed view of her
cheek and perfect nose and clear grey eyes, the stirring
had been less in his groin than in his chest, a kind of
lurching more than stirring, as if something were tugging
at his heart.

Which was impossible as he'd given up affairs of the
heart a long time ago, and found most of his companionship   and   physical   satisfaction   in   adventure
sports—'most' being the operative word!

'Thanks,' he said, belatedly letting go of her wrist and
realising he was repeating himself. Perhaps he'd better
get away from her for a while. Another swim?

Sam chose that moment to throw sand at him, a small
fistful hitting him squarely in the chest.

'Hey, you little monster,' he growled, and lunged at
the child, forgetting the baby barely knew him. Sam
shrieked and scrambled onto Sarah's lap, then shot him
such a look of triumph that Adam gave a shout of laughter.

'He's manipulative enough to be Fiona's child,' he
conceded, his smile lingering to encompass both Sam
and Sarah.

She smiled back at him and a swim became a necessity for him, his body reacting so strongly that to have
stayed would have been embarrassing.

Sarah watched enviously as he headed back into the
surf. The sun had disappeared behind the buildings that

lined the beach and the air was cooling quickly. It was too cold for Sam to swim but she wished she could fling her over-heated body into the waves and let the ocean wash away the silly longings and strange desires this man had stirred to life.

'It's because I haven't had a decent swim or surf since you came into my life,' she grouched to Sam. 'That's all.'

But could a longing for a swim explain the jittery feeling in her chest as Adam strode back up the beach? And would a good swim rid her of the palpitations his voice could cause at unexpected moments?

'Can I watch him while you have a dip?' he asked, his kindness once more apparent.

'He'll probably yell,' she said, wanting to go into the water so badly it hurt.

'So, let him yell,' Adam said easily. 'Look along the beach. Who'd hear him?'

The smile that accompanied his words had the power of a laser, easily piercing her skin to start both jiggling and palpitations. Cold water was definitely worth a try.

'I'm going for a swim and Adam's watching you,' she said to Sam, building a quick mound of sand to divert him while she departed.

He did yell, but she refused to listen and raced towards the water, leaping over the frilly bits close to the shore and then diving, as Adam had done, into the first green wave. The water cooled her skin and blood, making her tingle with well-being. How she'd missed the sea, the waves. Although she'd grown up in the country, with earth and air and sometimes fire, from her earliest beach holidays she'd recognised water as her preferred element, loving the rush it gave her and revelling in her mastery over it.

She rode three waves, body-surfing to shore and dash-
ing back after each one to maximise this unexpected
freedom. Then she reluctantly left the water, not wanting
to put either Sam or his minder under too much stress.

'You could have stayed longer,' Adam greeted her,
motioning towards Sam who was burrowing his fingers
into the sand and talking quite happily to himself.

'It was enough—really wonderful,' she assured him,
although the renewed vigour of the jiggling told her it
was also useless as a means of damping down attraction.

She felt the salt from the water drying on her body,
making her skin feel tight and raspy, and was aware of
the air, cool in her lungs. She towelled the excess water
from her hair and wondered if hormonal reactions made
nerve-endings more sensitive to their surroundings or if
it was the simple pleasure of relaxing on a beach that
was making her feel so alive.

'I'll go on up. I picked up a cot from Maggie as well
as the car-seat last night. Do you want it set up in the
bedroom you're using now or would you prefer him in
the other room?'

The switch from the magic of the beach to practicality
was difficult, and her thoughts stumbled against each
other.

'Perhaps in the same room,' she said hesitantly.
'There's no reason why we should spread ourselves all
through your house.'

'Feel free to do whatever is best,' he said stiffly, and
she knew that once again she'd broken the fine links of
the tenuous rapport between them.

'I'll come and give you a hand,' she suggested, and
this time his reply was a look of pure scorn.

'With that sandy baby perched on one hip? No,
thanks, I'll manage.'

He strode off up the beach, leaving Sarah to follow with the towels and the extremely sandy baby.

She reached the lawn area in time to see him turn off an outside shower. Well, at least she could wash the sand off herself and Sam before they went into the house and, hopefully, avoid another outburst from their host.

Puzzling over his sudden change from genial and kind to terse and sarcastic, Sarah shook sand off the towels then dropped them on the grass. Then she turned on the shower and stepped under the flow of warm water.

While Sam tried to catch the drops she closed her eyes, tipping her head back so the water ran across her face. Imprinted on her eyelids, she found an image of Adam's face, the close-up image she must have stored in her memory while she'd removed the grain of sand from his eye.

Would the image fade or would she return to Perth and find it there whenever she closed her eyes? Or would it come and go, reappearing with random disregard for her reactions to it, perhaps affecting her life for ever more?

CHAPTER SEVEN

BY THE time Sarah and Sam reached the bedroom one bed had been removed and the cot set up in its place. The plastic packs of nappies had been neatly stacked on a small side table and the formula and sterilising unit Sarah had bought today were on the table beneath the window.

The worker of these small miracles was also present, standing by the window as if she'd caught him surveying the completed job.

'The perfect host!' Sarah said dryly.

Adam bent his head in a gracious acceptance of her compliment.

'Look,' he said, 'I realise this probably isn't any easier for you than it is for me, but I can't do anything about your side of it. I'm flat out, trying to keep track of my own conflicting emotions.'

He paused and she waited tensely, completely at sea as to where this conversation might be leading.

'So could we pretend we're chance acquaintances? You could be a friend of someone in the family, staying here for a while. Perhaps that way we can stop sniping at each other.'

It was an offer of a truce, but Sarah was reluctant to accept it.

'I *am* a friend of someone in your family—or I was!' she muttered.

'And that's the kind of snipe I'm talking about!' He hit back at her so quickly she smiled.

115

'You're right,' she admitted, 'and I do understand what you're saying, but I don't think "snipe" is a noun.'

He grinned and she was sorry she'd agreed. Surely her heart would behave better if they kept fighting.

Sam put a halt to further conversation, by letting out a loud wail.

'He's hungry,' Sarah explained. 'I'd better get us dressed then do something about his dinner.'

This time Adam took the hint and left the room, but it seemed emptier without him. As she dressed herself and the child she made excuses for her heart's behaviour, but it was hard to believe that an absence of any form of social life for twelve months could be solely responsible for her condition. Or that any man, chance-met like this one, would have brought on the same physical symptoms.

A quick search of the suitcase failed to reveal the leather folder but perhaps it wasn't so important. She was beginning to believe a reference from God himself wouldn't mean much to Adam Fletcher.

In the kitchen she found the vegetables and meat she'd bought neatly put away in crisper dishes in the refrigerator. Setting Sam on the floor, she spread a few toys in front of him, then began to get his meal. He was obviously feeling more secure because he ignored the toys and crawled away from her to explore the big open room, not even scurrying back when Adam entered it a few minutes later.

The truce made for stilted conversation so when Adam offered her a drink Sarah responded far too enthusiastically.

'Gin and tonic, if you have it,' she said, lamely adding, when she realised her prompt reply might make him think she was an alcoholic, 'A small one.'

Not that the alcohol helped. In fact, it hindered, relaxing the bits of her that shouldn't be feeling warm and fuzzy while tightening the tension in her head.

Somehow she got the vegetables prepared, took out the chicken breasts and cut them into strips. She'd cut one strip finely, cook it and mix it in with Sam's vegetables, then later use the rest in a chicken and vegetable stir-fry for herself and Adam. She was wondering if she should ask him if he ate such things when the phone rang. He left the room, ignoring the extension near the kitchen bench and—to judge by the length of time it took him to answer it—going up to the top of the house to take the call.

When he returned he settled himself on a stool on the other side of the bench, sipping at his drink while he watched her work. The stilted conversation dried up. The silence became uncomfortable, charged with a new atmosphere now. She excused herself with the reminder that she'd never been good at light conversation or social chit-chat and concentrated on what she was doing, trying to ignore him.

Not easy!

Impossible, in fact. She was beginning to feel caged— like an animal in a zoo, with Adam Fletcher a customer who'd paid good money to come in and peer at her. Well, she was living in his house, so perhaps it wasn't such a bad analogy.

She glanced up at him, but he wasn't watching her at all. He had pulled a piece of paper from his pocket and was studying it, smoothing its surface as he read the words. Presumably he reread them as there didn't appear to be enough writing to hold his attention for more than a few seconds.

'Can I get you another drink?' he asked, lifting his

head so quickly she was sure he'd caught her watching him.

'No, thanks!' If warm and fuzzy was dangerous then becoming too warm and fuzzy could be downright disastrous. She walked out of the kitchen and bent over Sam, feeling Adam's gaze on her every move.

'Dinnertime,' she told the baby. 'We'll sit in the kitchen where we can confine your mess to a smaller area.'

He settled on the floor and she sat in front of him, pleased to be hidden from the silent watcher. Not that she had the relief for long. Sam ate quickly, polishing off the vegetables and then demolishing the stewed apples she'd also prepared for him. She stood up to rinse the cloth she'd used to wipe his face and found Adam watching her.

Closely. And, yes, the suspicion was alive and alert in his eyes.

'Is Sarah Tremayne your real name?'

The question snapped across the space between them, hitting her with the force of a fierce wind squall.

'Why are you asking?'

The moment the words were out of her mouth she knew it had been the wrong answer. A simple yes would have done, but it wouldn't have been simple or the complete truth.

'Why shouldn't I ask?' he demanded, the suspicion hardening to anger as she dodged the question. 'Wouldn't you want to know the identity of someone who'd conned their way into your home?'

Conned her way? Enough was enough!

She threw the cloth into the sink and settled her fists on her hips—it was a cliché of defiance but who cared?

'I did not con my way into your home,' she said,

speaking softly for Sam's sake but making certain every word reached its target. 'You insisted I came here. You ordered it! And, for your information, yes, Sarah Tremayne is my name. It's my professional name, the one I use as a nurse. If you'd like to run a check while I put Sam to bed, here's the phone number of the hospital where I worked.' She rattled off the code and eight digits. 'As I took leave without pay, I should still be listed as an employee.'

Her tirade completed, she bent, lifted Sam onto her hip and stalked out of the room. Then remembered she'd contracted to cook the meals. Turning back to Adam, she added, 'Your dinner will be ready at seven.'

It weakened her grand exit, but from the look on his face he hadn't been impressed by it anyway.

By the time Sam was asleep that was the least of her worries. The trouble with any kind of exit was that you eventually had to enter again so the re-entry became the problem. She'd never been able to sustain anger for very long so she didn't feel like marching in and demanding to know if he'd phoned the hospital.

And if he had, would their assurance that Sarah Tremayne was on leave have meant anything? Thinking it through, she'd realised that if she was the fake he thought her, she could have found the name of someone on leave and appropriated it in case this situation arose.

Aagh!

She didn't let the cry of frustrated anguish escape, smothering it to a muted groan as she washed her hands and face and brushed her hair. The reactive inner person, still traitorously attracted to the man who was causing all this turmoil, suggested putting on make-up.

Perhaps a little lip gloss wouldn't hurt.

She reached for the zipped pouch then pulled her hand away as if burnt.

Attracting him to her wasn't the answer—not that he'd be attracted to her. Hadn't Richard said he liked darkly beautiful women?

Maybe lip gloss would make *her* feel better.

This time she actually unzipped the pouch, before sighing loudly and zipping it back up. No, she'd wear no battle colours this evening, any more than she'd march in and make demands on him. She'd go quietly downstairs, cook their dinner, eat, then come back up to bed. Full stop. End of conversation. Get moving, Sarah.

Mentally prodding herself the whole way, she took the steps down to the living area. Adam was still sitting at the bench, the glass in front of him now empty.

As she made her way across the room, her legs stiff with the tension that held her body rigid, he looked up at her while his fingers again smoothed the paper.

'I've had confirmation that Fiona had a baby,' he said, and the sentence, which should have filled her with joy, sounded flat and lifeless in her ears.

'I'd already told you she'd had a baby,' she muttered at him as she opened the refrigerator and found the vegetables she wanted. 'Do you eat stir-fried chicken? Rice?'

He nodded, twice, and didn't try to hide the fact that he was watching her every move.

'My information says she and the baby were released into the care of a Sally Needham.'

'Your information?' The words faltered off her tongue. Had he had a private investigator looking into her life? She supposed it was his right so why did it make her feel sick?

She put a hand on the bench to steady herself and

took the three deep breaths she assured her patients would make them feel better. To a certain extent it worked—until Adam spoke again.

'I spoke to the policeman who handled Fiona's death—he checked it out for me.'

'Policeman?'

Adam shifted on his stool, wondering if he should move into the kitchen so he'd be ready to catch her if she fainted. She looked pale enough to faint—surely that must mean she was guilty of deceit.

Her fingers had tightened on the bench as she'd whispered the word, but now they relaxed and he realised she was recovering. It was time to strike, to add the other bit of information Bill Collins had given him. The single word—a title, in fact—which had struck him so forcibly that he'd gripped his own desk to steady himself.

Though why it should have mattered...

'Well?' he demanded, aware that this conversation wasn't going the way it had when he'd practised it in his head.

She looked up at him, her pupils so distended her eyes looked black in her pale face, then she looked away, turning her attention to the vegetables she'd arranged in a neat line on his bench-top.

'Sally Needham's my non-professional name,' she said, scraping at a carrot, her fingers shaking so much he couldn't watch.

He should hit her with the last bit, face her with the truth—throw the word at her and see how she managed to explain. He hesitated as he searched for the anger he'd felt earlier, needing it to bolster his attack. It was gone, blocked out by an image of those dark, beseeching eyes. Yet he had to bring out the one last piece of information, had to know. *Had* to know!

'Mrs Sally Needham?'

He emphasised the 'Mrs' just enough to give the question bite, but he was unprepared for the look of stark despair on Sarah's face. She bit her lip, her teeth pressing so tightly into one corner they must be drawing blood, then she straightened—metaphorically squaring her shoulders?—and looked into his eyes.

'I'm a widow,' she said, in such a cool, unemotional voice that he felt an icy shiver down his spine.

He looked at the bent head, saw the overhead light silvering the pale blonde hair, watched her fingers fumble with the carrot as she tried valiantly to peel it.

Unable to stand the sight of her distress any longer, he stood and walked around the end of the bench into the kitchen.

'Let me do that—you sit,' he ordered, taking the carrot from her, then putting his hands on her shoulders to steer her around to the stool he'd vacated.

He could feel her bones through the flesh on her shoulders—fragile bones, like a small bird's. Then they heaved and he realised she was crying, the movement a convulsive sob. Without conscious thought he turned her and held her pressed against his chest, moving his hands on her back and making soothing noises.

He moved the palm of his hand against the thin cotton of her T-shirt, imagining he could feel the frantic beating of her heart through skin and tissue and rib-cage.

Frightened by the intensity of his reaction to the thought, he lifted his hand and stroked her hair, telling himself all the time that he was offering comfort, nothing else—that this tearful reaction was more evidence of her guilt.

Then why wasn't he feeling triumph? Why was he

silently berating himself for upsetting her so badly, for reducing her to such frailty?

She pushed away from him, her hands pressing hard enough against his chest to make her intentions quite clear. Fishing in the pocket of her jeans, she produced a handkerchief like the one she'd used earlier to wipe the sand from his eye. He stood beside her, watching as she dried her tears and blew her small, neat nose.

She was still pale, but he sensed the tears had acted as a pressure valve, releasing the pent-up emotion his conversation had caused. But the name stuff had needed to be aired, he excused himself as she climbed onto the stool, rested her elbows on the bench-top and propped her chin on them.

'I don't usually cry,' she said bluntly, not exactly blaming him but adding to his own feeling of responsibility for her distress. 'In fact, I never cry!' she added defiantly. 'It must be tiredness from the train, but now it's over I feel fine. Do you want me to take over my duties again?'

'I make stir-fry for myself all the time,' he said, pleased to see her rally and hoping a normal conversation might undo a little of the harm. 'That's why I keep the electric wok out on the bench. You can cook some other night.'

But would she stay after all?

He frowned, wondering what he'd proved with his probing.

If her claim to both names was true, would having—using—two names make a person ineligible to adopt a child? And as for being married, hadn't he taunted her with wanting two parents for Fiona's child? But she wasn't married if she spoke the truth. She was a widow.

He stared at the badly mauled carrot in his hand, then

glanced up at her, checking the slim, ringless fingers which lay clasped on his bench.

'Do you want to talk about it?' he asked when the silence had become unbearable.

She looked up from her contemplation of her fingers and a small smile hesitated on her lips.

'About Fiona, having a baby, or me, using two names?' she asked him.

Her eyes challenged him to raise the third point, her husband's death, and although that had been exactly what he'd meant he couldn't bring himself to pick up that particular gauntlet.

She must have read defeat in his face because the smile became more real—cheekier, in fact—and she said, 'I suppose your next argument will be, "So, OK, she had a baby but how do I know Sam's that baby?" If he was a horse he'd have a passport with his distinguishing marks duly noted, but unfortunately he's only human and they don't note that kind of thing on birth certificates.'

Victory was helping her regain her strength, he realised, then wondered why he felt pleased. He'd always preferred to be a winner yet here he was, slicing vegetables and being pleased about defeat!

'Well, how do I know Sam's that baby?' he asked, taking the cue she'd offered him.

She frowned and he wanted to smooth the lines away, to see her smile again, but before he could analyse *that* reaction she was speaking again.

'That's my whole point. I brought it up yesterday. I don't see that it should matter to you whether he is or isn't. All you have to do is sign a letter, saying you're happy for me to adopt him. The fact that you're not certain he's Fiona's child should make it easier for you, not harder.'

He began to see it from her side, to see the logic in her argument. But, hell and damnation, she should be able to see his side as well.

'And if he is Fiona's? By signing my name, don't I accept your word that he is—then I give him away to a perfect stranger who takes him off to the other side of Australia and I never see him again? Could you do it if he was related to you?'

'I won't be a stranger,' she argued. 'That's why I agreed to stay here a month, and this is about the fourth time we've had this same argument. What happened to the truce?'

He saw colour in her cheeks and knew she'd recovered her composure. The colour made her look younger and prettier—too young to be a widow, too pretty to be unattached? He remembered how soft she'd felt in his arms—how well she'd fitted against his body—and wondered why he'd got himself into this mess. What freakish twist of fate had brought her through his clinic door?

He was slicing vegetables with deft, sure strokes, providing evidence that he'd done the job before. Sarah watched, wondering what he'd made of her sudden bout of tears—and of her answers to the questions which had caused them.

No, that was avoiding the truth. She hadn't cried for Colin but for herself. For some reason, being back at work—even if she didn't know what she was doing—and enjoying the companionship of other adults was making her life back home seem empty and forlorn.

She had Sam, of course, and for the past nine months it had seemed enough—more than enough. His company had been all she'd needed.

But now?

'What else do you eat?' she asked, locking away the weakness of such thoughts and trying for normal conversation, whatever that might be.

'Steak, salads, omelettes—not a lot of meat but more than I tell my prime athletes they should eat.'

'Isn't meat good for building muscle? Don't athletes need the amino acids in protein to build their strength?'

Her question won a smile but she controlled her internal reactions.

'Common misconception,' he said. 'Although people like weightlifters do have higher protein requirements, what an athlete needs most is energy—which comes from carbohydrates. And for the protein they do need meat isn't compulsory. For a long time people, even dietitians, believed animal protein was superior to vegetable protein, but that's now been disproved in myriad tests.'

'So no meat?' Sarah asked, hoping for another smile.

She got it and the jiggle became a flutter and moved to her lungs.

'Like everything else, they need a balanced amount of it. The problem with animal protein, particularly beef, is the high fat and kilojoule content in it. Beans will give an athlete the protein he or she needs, plus carbohydrates and fibre, but without the fat. Did I show you the diet sheets for the swimmers?'

Sarah shook her head, then remembered something she'd meant to bring up earlier.

'I think we got sidetracked but, while we're talking about them, one of the girls—Narelle her name was—had extremely low body fat. Below the fifteen per cent recommended as minimum for women. Is it something you'd take a look at?'

He was pouring a minute quantity of oil into the wok as she spoke, and spun to face her.

'Do you think she's anorexic?' he demanded.

Sarah shifted on the stool, uncomfortable now he'd put her fear into words.

'Maybe not,' she said. 'A lot of young women are naturally very thin, and I suppose if she's been doing any swimming training at all it could accentuate her problem.'

'I'll have a look at her,' Adam promised, turning his attention back to cooking. 'Remind me when they next come in. Tomorrow, isn't it?'

He threw the chicken pieces in the pan then asked about the other body-fat measurements. Had any been excessively high for their weight and age? Had she picked up any other anomalies?

It led to a discussion on the need for body fat and Sarah found herself relaxing. When Adam asked if she'd like a glass of white wine with her meal she agreed, wanting to hold the mood of camaraderie as long as possible.

If this was how a truce felt, long may it last, she decided as she stood up to clear their plates.

'You cooked so I'll clear up,' she said, as he stood and followed her to the kitchen.

'I can help,' he retorted. 'It's my house so I can make the rules.'

Was it the reminder of his ownership—his current domination of her life—that changed the mood or was it his body in her space again? Too close for comfort!

He opened a drawer and pulled out a teatowel, then stood expectantly beside her, obviously waiting for her to wash so he could dry the dishes.

Her mind screamed a silent protest while her body

longed to sway against him, remembering how hard his had felt when he'd held her as she'd cried.

She ran water in the sink, found detergent and added it, then plunged her hands into the frothy suds, hoping to hide the trembling of what she imagined was desire.

Had she ever felt like this with Colin? Wanting him so badly her body shook? Surely she'd remember if she had.

'Perhaps—'

'Perhaps?'

She glanced at him, pleased she'd stopped the rest of the sentence she hadn't meant to say aloud.

Perhaps her body hadn't been mature enough to feel like this, she'd been thinking. At eighteen she'd barely begun to grow breasts!

'I was thinking out loud,' she said, hoping he'd accept the excuse and take over the conversation.

'I can think of some perhaps, too,' he said softly, and she gripped the plate she was washing more tightly and willed her body to behave.

This was definitely not the kind of conversation she'd had in mind, but it was all he'd offered so she'd better run with it.

'Like, ''Perhaps I'll sign the paper after all and you can head back to Perth tomorrow''?' she tried.

He chuckled and the throaty noise lingered in his words. 'Anxious to escape me, Sarah?'

Her name sounded huskily in her ears and she felt the heat of his body as if he'd shifted closer to her.

'Perhaps I'm anxious to be home.'

'Are you?'

He was definitely closer for the words brushed seductively across her skin.

'Perhaps,' she said weakly, and tried to move away.

Her feet seemed weighted down with bricks and her body will-less as his fingers gently clasped her chin and turned her head so he could look into her eyes.

His own were bright. With the teasing laughter she'd seen before or something else? She couldn't tell, but she couldn't tear her gaze from his either, mesmerised by the blueness and the messages she didn't understand.

'Perhaps?' he echoed, studying her with an intensity which should have made her squirm but instead started fires burning, low down in her belly, setting up an ache there and a tingling in her nipples.

'I'll have to go home some time,' she said desperately, but she didn't pull away from the light grip of those fingers or move from the seductive circle of desire his body had enclosed around her.

'Perhaps!' he said, and she imagined she heard regret in his voice, but she had little time to think about it for he bent his head and brushed a kiss across her lips. Light as thistledown, potent as poison.

'I've some calls to make. Perhaps you can finish drying up,' he said, straightening as abruptly as he'd bent his head, then turning on his heel and marching out of the room. He'd cast her adrift from his presence so suddenly she had to clutch at the bench to stay upright.

Sarah took another three deep breaths, then one more for luck, waiting for the tumult in her senses to abate enough for her to think.

He was teasing her. She knew that for certain because he'd used the word 'perhaps' again. Teasing her with her own uncertainty.

'We'll see about that, Dr Adam Fletcher!' she stormed, grabbing the abandoned teatowel and polishing a wet plate furiously. 'Don't think you can kiss me and get away with it.'

But even said aloud, edged with tight-lipped anger, the threat didn't carry the conviction she'd have liked to hear.

It was hard to be convincing when inside she knew how alive the fleeting touch of his lips had made her feel—and that what she'd like more than anything would be for Adam to kiss her again.

The thought was ominous enough to block her mind completely so she finished the dishes, cleaned up the kitchen and scurried thankfully out of the room.

She'd left the lamp alight on the table by the window, and in its muted glow she could see Sam, sleeping peacefully, his dreams untroubled by the chaos he was causing her.

She looked at the single bed beside the cot, thinking she should be tired. It should be calling to her. The idea of going to bed, even with the added inducement of finishing the book she'd been reading on the train, didn't hold any appeal. She was too wired to sleep, her body still fizzing with the aftermath of the kiss, her muscles tight with the denial of its power.

She slid open the glass doors and stepped out onto the balcony beyond the room. She felt the dampness of the sea air hit her skin and relished the coldness of the night. She moved towards the railing and saw her shadow move in the rectangle of yellow light the lamp was throwing on the beach. Then she saw another shadow move, and knew that someone was on the balcony above her.

Adam?

Probably! Unless he'd smuggled his girlfriend into the house while his guest had been cleaning the kitchen.

The thought made her smile, easing some of her tension.

'Does it look the same from your side of the continent—the moonlight on the water?'

'Just the same,' she told him, relieved to hear her voice sounded as calm and even as his had. 'Of course, I feel I'm upside down—my sense of direction is all haywire because the sea is in the wrong place.'

'Join the club,' he said softly, 'although it's not the sea that's thrown me out of plumb.'

She was puzzling over his words when the shadow moved again and was gone. The upper square of light was now complete—unbroken as the silence that descended once again.

Only it wasn't silent. The waves washed up the beach, shh-ing each other, and somewhere the breeze sang along a wire, high-pitched but cheerful. Night sounds, muted by the darkness. As Sarah listened the square of light, shining from above, disappeared and she fancied she heard a footfall on the steps. Seconds later a car engine growled to life, and she heard the far-off but still recognisable sound of the garage door, opening.

Had his phone calls included one to a lady friend? Was he heading off to practise kissing somewhere else?

Not that it made the slightest difference to her what he did, she told herself firmly, but the night had lost its magic, the wind in the wires now sobbing out a sad refrain.

CHAPTER EIGHT

THE truce, uneasy though some aspects of it were, must have been working, Sarah decided. They'd managed to get through to the end of the first week, three whole days, then a weekend, not spent together as Adam had gone diving, and now another week—bringing them to Friday again—since its declaration.

She had met a multitude of patients and was getting to know the swimmers as friends as well as patients. She hadn't met his mother or his grandmother but had learnt they'd left on a cruise a few days after she'd arrived. Had he hustled them away so he could worry over the Sam-decision on his own or so he wouldn't have to explain Sarah's presence in his house? Or had they been booked to go anyway—a coincidence that, no doubt, had suited Adam?

She didn't ask and he didn't tell her. Nor did he ask any more about her marriage, although everything else about her life in Perth was fair game for a bit of probing.

Keeping busy had helped the truce remain intact. It hadn't taken her long to become fascinated with the range of patients Adam saw or be drawn into the sport-related injuries and illnesses he treated.

Every evening she took home a textbook on strapping, learning the intricacies of applying tape to injured joints and muscles and the basic principles behind the technique.

'Does it interest you more than other aspects of my

work?' Adam had asked when she first borrowed the book.

'Not really,' she'd told him, 'but it seems I can be of more real help to you if I learn the different techniques. I always knew the idea behind strapping is to build a bridge from the uninjured tissue over the injured part, but each area has such specific needs I thought I'd study it. And it's coming in useful,' she'd reminded him. 'I did a dislocated finger today, strapping it on the splint in the flexed position. I wouldn't have been able to do it if I hadn't been reading the book while I watched the reception desk at lunchtime.'

He'd hesitated, as if considering his next comment, but in the end he hadn't replied. He'd simply observed her in silence for a moment then headed back to his office, muttering to himself about something—the only word she'd caught being 'usefulness'.

After that brief conversation he'd turned the swimmers' training over to her, showing her the exercises on the equipment and leaving her to monitor their progress. It made her feel she was doing real work and she soon became involved in their improvement.

Together they'd worked out how to approach Narelle about her low body fat and below-average weight. They'd seen her together, their combined persuasive skills necessary for her to agree to try to stick to the diet Adam prescribed, using improvement in her swimming times as the carrot and the threat of early onset osteoporosis as the stick to make her eat more.

'If her body fat measurements don't improve we'll get a professional counsellor in to talk to her. Anorexia nervosa is a psychoneurotic disorder and needs skilled treatment,' Adam had said when Narelle had left the room.

Sarah remembered the conversation as she waited for

Adam to finish with his last patient—a weightlifter with bicipital tendinitis. She'd already looked up the injury— small tears in the tendons where they passed over the top of the humerus, causing pain whenever the poor guy lifted a weight. She'd even checked on the treatment, which started with the inevitable RICE, an acronym for most sprains and strains, as common in this world as ABC was in emergency medicine.

Rest—how many dedicated sportsmen or women took notice of that one? Ice—well, they all used ice to reduce swelling, then they probably went straight back into training or competing. Compression—that's where the strapping techniques came in, an alternative being to wrap an elastic bandage around the injury to prevent fluid accumulating at the site. The E was for elevation, but shoulders were already elevated above chest level so this fellow would have to go with RIC today.

Having sorted out the patient's problems, she thought about the feeling of unity that working with Adam and Jane had given her. She'd chosen midwifery as her special field, but now realised her work at the huge maternity section of a public hospital had lacked the ongoing contact with patients and staff which she was enjoying at the clinic. In the labour ward the women passed through, most staying in hospital only a few days. Obs and Gynae specialists came and went, bustling in and out at odd hours of the day and night, staff changed each shift and there was little sense of being part of a team, let alone valued.

Not that Adam had mentioned the word 'valued' in connection with her. He was still thinking more on the lines of 'nuisance' and 'problem', still eyeing her with suspicion.

Their evenings had also fallen into a pattern. Most

days they were home early enough for Sam to have a play on the beach. Adam would swim, then mind the baby while Sarah dived and surfed. She relished these times, and told herself it was the swim and the short time of freedom from the responsibility of Sam which meant so much to her. It had nothing to do with Adam's presence on the same patch of sand or the silly jiggling of her heart and unlikely dreams of family that crept into her head at this time of the day.

'Daydreaming? Thinking of home?'

Adam spoke but Sam saved her answering. He had come to regard Adam as a favoured person and made a bee-line for him at every opportunity. His insistent demands to be picked up and swung onto those broad shoulders blotted out anything Sarah might have said and diverted Adam's attention.

She was pleased the baby had taken to his uncle, less pleased about the obvious affection Adam showed to Sam. The question of the final consent was one that niggled in the back of Sarah's mind all the time, although these days her reactions to the man causing this concern often overshadowed it. Perhaps it was time to ask again about his signature, get her priorities straight!

When he'd buckled Sam into his car-seat. Or perhaps over dinner tonight. If Adam was home...

Wishing and hoping, but for what?

It would be safer with him gone, but her heart denied common sense.

She had a bet with herself that he wouldn't be home, not tonight and not for the weekend. Was he deliberately keeping out of her way so she couldn't badger him about Sam's adoption?

The thought made her sit up straighter. Forget the heart stuff—you're here on business, Sarah.

'So, what are you doing tonight?' she asked, as he drove them homeward.

He glanced her way, his raised eyebrows asking for further explanation.

'Well, this week I've had a chance to see the full programme—Monday night, touch football training, Tuesday night Harriers, Wednesday night was squash and Thursday the touch game. I wondered what you do on Fridays when you don't go off on a diving weekend?'

Repeating the question—in detail—made Sarah feel uneasy. In fact, she'd been relieved—well, more relieved than disappointed—when he'd explained his programme and told her he wouldn't eat with her most nights, preferring to fix himself a meal after sport rather than eat before it.

'Basketball,' he said, interrupting her thoughts. 'Yes, basketball on Fridays.'

This time disappointment won hands down!

'And the weekend?' she asked with a sugar-coated sweetness. 'Cricket? Or is that too slow for you? White-water rafting, perhaps?'

Another sidelong glance.

'Too cold this time of the year—the best rivers are further south. In autumn and winter I stick to hiking or rock-climbing.'

'I was actually joking,' she said, gazing at him in disbelief. 'No one can be so involved in sport that it fills all their off-duty hours—well, all your on-duty ones as well. That's not interest, that's addiction.'

Too late she realised she'd said a word which should have remained unsaid. Now it throbbed in the air of the car and tapped at Sarah's temple. She clutched her hands together in her lap and waited for Adam's reaction. Explosion?

And waited.

He'd steered the car into the garage and shut off the engine before he replied.

'I've never thought of it that way, but I suppose it could be,' he said quietly, staring out through the windscreen towards the blank wall ahead of them. 'Except that I believe I use sport for the physical and mental pleasure it gives me. Testing myself against mountains, pushing my body to its limits, mentally meeting the challenges of whatever game I happen to be playing.'

Sam was quiet and Sarah turned to see that he'd fallen asleep. She wanted to get out of the car, away from the uneasy atmosphere her question had generated, but couldn't use the excuse of a fidgety baby.

'But is it a balanced life?' Adam continued, and she guessed he was leading the conversation along some pre-set path. 'And is yours any more balanced? You're a young woman yet you've tied yourself to a baby you didn't bear and, from what I can gather from your not-too-revealing conversation, he's become the focal point of your existence. Is that healthy?'

'He's been sick,' Sarah argued weakly. 'That's the only reason he needed more attention.'

'You seem to enjoy the work at the clinic. Had you found yourself missing your career? Regretting your decision to devote yourself to Sam?'

'Would I have come here if I had?' she demanded, rising hotly to the bait.

'Possibly,' he said, 'if you had some agenda of your own for wanting to adopt him.'

The words chilled her. Had he received more information from his tame policeman or had it been a shot in the dark? Not that it was an agenda. More a safeguard. And security for Sam.

'Well, I haven't and for your information I've enjoyed being a full-time carer for him. As for a career...'

She stopped, her heart thudding as she realised she'd been about to say out loud the very thing she had trouble admitting to herself. That nursing had been a means of escape from loneliness and grief. That it had provided what she'd needed at the time but had remained too un-focussed for her to class it as a career.

Adam watched her thoughts cast shadows on her face. He'd have loved to know what she'd been about to say but experience had taught him that Sarah didn't let much slip past her guard. Perhaps he should have stayed home more in the evenings, instead of finding excuses to be out, but that first—and only—meal together had shaken him. It had made him think of family and see her as a woman—two complications he'd prefer to continue to avoid.

'As for a career?' He said the words quietly, prompting her but not pressuring her for a response.

She shrugged, the slim shoulders with the fragile bones lifting then dropping.

'I forget what I was going to say,' she lied, a faint flush on her cheeks telling him he'd read it correctly.

Perhaps he should stay home tonight and try to find out more about her life, her past—the husband! Of course he should, but would he? Dared he risk it?

A disgruntled cry from Sam put a stop to his specu-lation. It was amazing how quickly he'd learnt to inter-pret the child's noises. This one meant, 'What am I do-ing sitting in this car-seat when I should be at the beach?'

Chuckling at his stupid thoughts, he got out of the car, opened the back door and felt his heart clench as the baby smiled and held his hands towards him. Another complication! By avoiding her outside working hours, he could probably keep a lid on his growing attraction to Sarah, but how did he prevent an infant creeping under his defences, breaching the barriers against love he'd erected so carefully when Fiona had run away?

'OK, mate,' he told the little boy. 'I'll take you to the beach while Sarah gets changed.'

Sarah watched him walk away, with Sam babbling happily in his arms. She ignored the stab of jealousy, reminding herself that Sam's life had been too restricted for too long. She headed to her bedroom, stripped off, showered and pulled on her swimming costume. Through the window she could see Adam and Sam, both dark heads bent over some intricate construction job.

She looked beyond them to the ocean, where the surf was whipped up by a south-easterly. The surfers were enjoying the bigger waves. A group of six youngsters, by the size of them, were paddling out, then turning and sitting on their boards as they waited for the perfect wave.

That's what you need, she told herself A couple of hours on a surfboard to make you remember the sheer joy of living. Perhaps Adam had a board tucked away in one of the storerooms at the rear of the garage. She'd ask him.

Buoyed by the thought of being on a board again, she headed downstairs, across the front lawn and onto the beach. From the top of the dune she could see the riders again, paddling to catch a curling wall of water, all six standing, balancing, flying forward until the churning backwash met them and dumped them all unceremoniously into the water.

She knew that feeling, too—frustration and the panic as you tried to find your board again before it was swept out of reach up onto the beach where you had to retrieve it then paddle all the way back out again.

There was one rider up again, three, five—where was number six? The surfers must have done a head count for she could see their gestures, their bodies turning as they searched for a sign of their mate. The sixth board was already beached and she was running before she'd realised it.

Adam shouted something as she sped past but she couldn't distinguish the words, her whole being focussed on the spot where the boy had disappeared. As she dived she saw one of the other boys diving also, his mate holding his board for him. She swam underwater near the sand, knowing there was less resistance there, and surfaced near the boards.

'Joey didn't come up,' a young lad told her. He was sitting on his board and had the ankle straps of another two held firmly in his hand. 'Pete and Finn are looking for him.'

The pair surfaced at that moment, the limp form of their friend held awkwardly between them. Blood streamed from a gash near his temple, brilliant red on his chalk-white face.

'We'll get him to the beach,' Sarah said, lifting him, with the help of his friends, onto one of the boards. If you can, without endangering yourself, start resuscitation! The words were imprinted in her mind. She pedalled her legs to keep her body upright in the water, and turned Joey's head towards her. Steadying herself with one hand on the board, she gripped his nostrils closed, fitted her mouth over his and gave him five quick breaths.

'Wave coming!' The glad cry gave them all hope. Sarah hesitated. If she stayed in the water and kept breathing for him the wave could tip him off the board, whereas if they caught the wave she'd have the lad on the beach in seconds. She hauled herself up onto the board and knelt there, praying her body would remember what to do as she rode with her injured cargo into shore.

'Yes!'

She heard the exultant shout as the wave lifted them and the board surged forward. She steadied the lad with both hands as it speared towards the beach, wondering if the lack of oxygen in the boy's blood—hypoxaemia— was severe enough to have stopped his heart beating. The blow on his head must have knocked him unconscious, and he'd taken water into his lungs. His body's own defence mechanisms had then started shutting things down.

Adam, stripped to his underpants, was waiting in the shallows. Sam was on the dry sand a little further up the beach, too interested in the excitement to complain of his neglect.

Sarah saw Adam's hand close around the boy's wrist, then feel for a pulse beneath his jaw.

'You,' he barked, turning to the lad who'd caught the same wave in to shore, 'go up to that house. There's a phone on a table in the downstairs room. Dial triple O and get an ambulance here as soon as possible.' He'd lifted the boy off the board and was carrying him up the beach as he finished the order.

After checking that Sam was safe, Sarah knelt beside the lad and watched as Adam gripped his nose and gave four quick breaths into his lungs.

'Chest's rising so there's no obstruction,' she said, as Adam removed his mouth to allow the air to escape naturally.

Once again he tried for a pulse, Sarah counting off five seconds before he turned to her again.

'There's no pulse so I'll do the chest compressions. You breathe for him. Do you know the count?'

Sarah nodded, pleased someone else had taken control. She could have done it quite competently, but her hands would have shaken as she'd measured the correct position on the tanned but bony chest and Adam's strength would mean more successful compression.

She counted in her head—one one-thousand, two one-thousand—and matched her pace to Adam's movement, leaning forward to close the nostrils and breathe air into the stubborn lungs on every fifth count.

In between breaths she rolled her shirt into a pad and pressed it against the head wound. She checked for a pulse, willing the boy's heart to resume beating—praying his youth and resilience would save him.

'Pulse!' she shouted, overjoyed to feel the beat, overwhelmed to see a pink flush spread slowly into the clammy white skin.

Adam's fingers brushed hers aside, and at that moment the boy jerked convulsively, rolled to one side and gagged then vomited sea water.

'Get the towels. We'll need to warm him now,' Adam snapped, and Sarah stepped over Sam, who'd crawled down the beach to watch their progress, and hurried to do his bidding. OK, so it was good to have someone in control, but did he have to be so brusque with his orders?

A shout from the house told her the ambulance had arrived, and as she wrapped towels around the shivering youth she saw the two attendants, hurrying down the beach, incongruous in their trim uniforms and shiny black shoes but so welcome they could have been naked for all she cared.

One carried a lightweight stretcher, folded in half for easy mobility, while the other had a backpack slung across his shoulder. She knew it would have an oxy-viva in it, drugs and fluid to restore the surfer's electrolyte balance and, among an assortment of other things, a portable defibrillation unit. She shivered, pleased they hadn't needed to shock the lad's heart back to life. As a nurse she'd only seen it happen a few times, but the convulsive effect on the patient's body, particularly a child's, had frightened her.

She moved out of the way, picking up Sam, and held him tight, his life doubly precious when one had so nearly been lost. Behind her she could hear Adam's voice as he questioned the other lads, organising them. She turned to him.

'Do you want me to contact his parents? They could meet the ambulance at the hospital.'

He frowned at her, as if surprised she had the brains to think of such a thing.

'No need. He lives a little further along the beach and his young brother ran straight home. I think that's his mother, coming now.'

He nodded towards a woman, racing along the sand, and sent one of the other lads to meet her and tell her the boy was OK. Knowing there was nothing more she could do and feeling strangely flat after the adrenalin rush of the rescue, Sarah walked up towards the house. She paused under the shower to wash the sand off herself and Sam, then hurried up to their room, silently apologising for dripping on the tiles as their towels were still wrapped around the patient.

She was in the kitchen, preparing dinner for Sam, when Adam reappeared, his scowling frown still in place.

'What on earth possessed you to race out there to help that boy?' he demanded.

Sarah was staggered, so much so that she opened her mouth and shut it again several times before she finally responded. 'I should have let him drown?' she asked, sweetness masking her anger.

'No, of course not, but his friends would probably have got him in or they could have shouted. I'd have gone.'

'Five minutes later? Ten?' she queried, and now he caught the deception and turned away. He thrust his hand through his hair, scratched a little then turned back to face her.

'OK, I'm reacting badly. Your quick response possibly, no, probably, saved his life—certainly gave us a better chance of resuscitating him. But, well, you put yourself at risk. The surf was wild out there. You could have been injured, struck on the head by one of the boards—'

'Is that what's bugging you? Two people to rescue instead of one? I'm sorry you thought you'd be inconvenienced.'

Sam must have heard the sarcasm in her voice for he crawled towards her, then looked at Adam, decided he'd do instead and moved towards him to sit on his foot. So much for loyalty!

'It isn't that...'

The man was actually stumbling over his words and leaving his sentences half-finished. She'd have liked to ask him what it was, then, but didn't have the nerve, taking pity on him instead.

'I'm sorry if it bothered you, but it was an instinctive reaction,' she explained. 'I spent all my summers at the beach and was a Nipper—junior lifesaver. Then, when

I was old enough, I became a fully fledged member of the fraternity—surfboard rescues a speciality!'

She sketched a curtsy, then turned her attention back to Sam's dinner. For some reason the bald statement of facts she'd thought would clear the air had made things worse. She could feel tension coiling around the room, like wisps of steam escaping from a cauldron.

'What about Sam?' Adam demanded. 'What would have happened to him if you'd been—injured?'

Sarah stared at him. He'd been going to say 'killed'— she knew it as certainly as if he'd pronounced the word.

'This conversation is ridiculous,' she said coldly. 'I wasn't injured—or killed. Nor was I likely to be. I take your point about Sam, and I would never knowingly put myself at risk while he's totally dependent on me. In fact, it's to protect him, in case I'm accidentally killed, that I want to make him legally mine through adoption. Does that answer your question?' She glared at him. 'And aren't you due at a basketball game?'

Again he ran his fingers through his hair and stood there, staring at her. He looked so uncertain she wondered if he was suffering from a delayed reaction to the rescue. This wasn't the organised authoritarian with whom she usually shared the house or the man who'd snapped his orders on the beach. What had caused the change?

She waited, knowing there was something more he had to say, but when the words came they were so unexpected it took her a minute to process them.

'I was worried about you—terrified, in fact. And I'm not going to basketball.'

By the time she was certain of what she'd heard, he'd left the room, leaving only the echo of his footsteps as he walked up the stairs.

He returned as Sam was eating his egg custard.

'Isn't there some kind of chair arrangement for babies to sit in to be fed?' he demanded.

Back to normal again, Sarah thought as she looked up—and up. He'd come into the kitchen where she and Sam were in their usual dinner position on the floor, and he seemed to tower over her. Not that she was going to be intimidated by a bit of towering.

'High chair,' she said succinctly. 'I didn't think it was worth getting one for so short a stay, and I'm not confident enough of his balance to put him on an ordinary chair so this is the next best solution.'

She shifted her attention back to Sam and continued to feed him as she explained, that one look at Adam enough to convince her that looking at him this evening wasn't a good idea. He was dressed to go out—not in the long silky shorts a basketballer might wear but in smart casual clothes. Very smart casual clothes.

The trousers, judging by what she could see within her limited range of vision, were gaberdine, beautifully pressed, a drab fawn colour. From the glimpse she'd had of his shirt, it was either silk or some other material with a dull sheen. It was fine enough to cling lightly and lovingly to his muscles so, from her viewpoint, his shoulders looked immense.

'I'll get one tomorrow.' The words snapped across her head. 'It's ridiculous for you to be sitting on the floor to feed him.'

'Well, your mood didn't improve under the shower,' Sarah said, more to herself than to him but loud enough for him catch her comment if he chose.

'My mood is perfectly friendly,' he said. 'Has Sam finished his dinner? Is he going to bed now?'

Puzzled by his questions, Sarah looked up again, but

her view of his face was restricted to the stubbornly tilting chin. Which told her nothing new. She'd known from day one about his stubbornness.

She wiped Sam's face then stood, bending to lift him onto her hip in the same movement.

'Why?'

He seemed disconcerted by her question, but no more so than she felt. Adam Fletcher in jeans and T-shirts, or in aging sports gear, caused serious enough heart problems, but this well-dressed version was so stunning he stole the air from her lungs.

'Going out?' she mumbled, forgetting it was his turn in the conversation. 'Somewhere special?'

Now her heart was aching, pulsing with its familiar reaction to him but hurting at the same time. The men she knew didn't get dressed up like this to go out with the boys. No, this man was dressed for a date!

'That depends,' he said. There was no humour in his voice and she imagined, for all his bossiness, a rare uncertainty in his eyes. 'I've phoned Jacinta and she's coming over to babysit. I thought we might have dinner together.'

Sarah's heart was overjoyed but her head knew it was a far from sensible idea.

'We could have dinner together every night of the week if you didn't go rushing out somewhere,' she said.

'Yes, but it didn't seem such a good idea at the time.'

She repeated the words in her head, but they still didn't make much sense so she gave them back to him.

'And is this?' she asked, adding, when he looked bewildered by her question, 'Such a good idea?'

'Probably not,' he admitted, 'but you've seen nothing of the area—haven't been beyond this house, the beach and my clinic.'

'So it's a politeness thing—showing the visitor around?' she asked, wondering why she should suddenly feel depressed.

'Not entirely,' he said stiffly. 'Now, do you want to come or don't you?'

The brisk demand proved he'd lost the uncertainty he'd had—or she'd imagined. He was back to his old 'control freak' self.

'OK,' Sarah replied, shrugging one shoulder at the same time to show it was no big deal, while her heart pounded with excitement and her head told her she was mad.

'Good. Now, get Sam to bed and as soon as Jacinta arrives we can be off.'

Sarah looked at him then glanced down at her baggy sweatpants.

'Oh, yeah?' she said, and left the room.

Adam headed for the small bar fridge in the corner of the living room. He needed a drink—even if it was only a soft drink—after that ordeal. Did all women put a man through the third degree before they'd agree to go out or was it only this particular one he was harbouring under his roof?

And what had her question meant? Was she reneging on her agreement?

No, a soft drink wouldn't do. He definitely needed a beer to think about that one. He pulled out a can of low-alcohol beer, figuring he could then have a glass or two of wine with dinner and still be under the limit for driving home.

He snapped the top and took a long pull of it, then wandered out onto the balcony and sat down, looking out to sea. He decided that maybe he hadn't handled things too badly after all.

He was working out his possible alcohol intake if he had a second can when his house-guest returned. Well, he assumed it was his house-guest, although there was little superficial resemblance between the woman who wore T-shirts and jeans or baggy sweatpants all day and this vision who had just glided across his living-room floor.

Her hair was caught up on top of her head somehow, but bits of it had escaped and were wisping around her temples and trailing down the soft skin at her nape.

'You didn't have to get dressed up!' he mumbled, wondering how he'd control his hands once he was within touching distance of her. There seemed to be so much of her to touch—her skin so white against the stark black of the dress she'd poured herself into, white shoulders, shoulder-blades, the curving fullness at the top of her breasts.

He forced his attention away from her breasts and inadvertently found her legs. No visible skin there, thankfully, but her black stockings were nearly as magnetic. His fingers tingled with a desire to smooth the blackness—

'No, I thought not.' She smiled sweetly and let her gaze run over his attire, reminding him that he'd dressed for the occasion. 'But I'd thrown a dress into my bag at the last minute and thought I'd give it an airing.'

'That's a dress?' he floundered, trying for cool and casual humour. In fact, she'd thrown in a pair of wickedly sexy black, high-heeled sandals as well and they were making him think things he shouldn't be thinking. Cool was a long way off!

She smoothed the skirt so it crept another quarter of an inch down her shapely thigh, drawing attention to her legs rather than making them less obvious.

'Well?' she asked, and he tried to remember what they'd been talking about.

'Well, what?'

'Is Jacinta here? Shall we go?' She spoke slowly, the way people spoke to young children or foreigners who might not have understood.

He was about to repeat 'Jacinta' but caught himself in time. No wonder she was treating him as if he was half-witted. It was how he felt.

The pealing of the doorbell saved his sanity.

'That's her now. I'll let her in and show her around. Would you like a drink while you're waiting?'

Sarah shook her head, sending more of the little wispy bits of hair loose to frame her face and emphasise the delicate beauty of it.

He crushed his beer can in one fist, first checking surreptitiously that it had been light not heavy beer. No, it wasn't alcohol confusing him.

'I won't be long,' he added inanely, then headed down the steps.

CHAPTER NINE

ADAM had booked a table at Grumpy's, and as he drove north along the highway towards the restaurant he decided that hadn't been a good idea. It was bad enough to sit in the car with her, smelling her skin—or was it a very subtle perfume? If he added moonlight to the equation—and the tides were full so he'd bet his life there'd be a big moon—and the silvered sheen of the Broadwater, a man could lose his head.

'Shouldn't you be pointing out the sights?' Sarah asked, the slight huskiness of her voice breaking into his chaotic thoughts.

'Sights?'

'I thought you'd asked me out so I could see something of the place. Did I get it wrong? Is this a business dinner? Are we going to talk about Sam and you signing a letter for me?'

He swallowed the groan that rose in his throat and threatened to choke him. How could what had seemed so sensible turn so awkward?

He sneaked a look towards her and saw her lovely profile and the sweet tilt of her lips. It was her fault, damn it. If she hadn't put on that dress and fiddled with her hair everything would have been all right.

'That's the Marriot Hotel,' he said, belatedly for he was already swinging right across the southbound highway, heading for the Spit with its first-class hotels and restaurants and the Sea World adventure park.

He pointed out the yacht club and explained how the

river emptied into a wide expanse of water, the Broadwater, protected from the sea by a long, thin strip of sand and further north by a sand island. Then his conversation dried up as he turned into the car park. He had an uneasy feeling that he wasn't going to enjoy walking into a restaurant with Sarah Tremayne. Not this Sarah Tremayne, who would turn the heads of both men and women.

Which raised another puzzle to occupy his mind. Normally he felt proud, being seen with an attractive woman—in fact, he made a point of it, keeping up friendly relations with a number of local beauties.

So why did he want to wrap his old picnic blanket around Sarah and hustle her past the other diners?

'Is this it?' she asked, and he turned towards her. He'd been right about the moon. It was already reflecting off the water, shining far enough into the car to make her hair look silver and enhance the ethereal appearance he'd noticed the first day they'd met.

'Yes,' he said, but he made no move to get out. Perhaps if he sat here long enough she'd suggest they went home.

Unable to bear the tension in the car a moment longer, Sarah felt for the doorhandle and released the lock. Pushing it open, she got out, then caught a glimpse of the water between the buildings. Drawn irresistibly towards it, she shut the door and walked slowly away from the vehicle. Adam could please himself!

There was a marina beyond the restaurant complex, and boats rocked quietly against their padded moorings. Further out, houseboats dotted the placid water, and an occasional shout came from fishermen in dinghies. It was a scene of such tranquil beauty that Sarah felt it touch her soul.

Surely everything will be all right! Could things go badly wrong again in a place of such serenity?

She knew he'd followed her, her skin alert to every move when he was near her.

'Like it?' he said quietly, coming to stand beside her and resting one hand on her shoulder. There was no possession in the touch, nothing more than friendliness, but its warmth sent music singing through her body, melodies and heat in equal measure.

'It's beautiful,' she murmured, afraid to break the spell the moonlight had woven around them.

'Very beautiful,' he agreed, and his fingers touched a tendril of her hair, making her wonder if he was talking about the scenery.

They stood a little longer, then he took her hand and led her inside. They went up the stairs, following the receptionist, out to a table on the balcony that overlooked the moonlit water.

By some unspoken agreement, they set their circumstances aside and talked first of the choices offered by the menu, then seafood in general and their likes and dislikes. The conversation led naturally to wine—they both enjoyed a dry white—and they settled, when the waiter came, on a Houghton's white burgundy.

'A West Australian wine. Have you visited the vineyards?' Adam asked, and for a split second Sarah hesitated, knowing this was the opportunity to tell him a little about herself yet not wanting to break the spell the moon had cast upon them.

'Most of them,' she admitted. 'I enjoy tasting different wines and buying a couple of bottles of the ones I fancy, particularly wine I think might improve with age. It's a challenge.'

'Do you go often?' he asked, and she looked into his

eyes and saw only interest, not interrogation. He smiled at her as if to confirm the innocence of the question and she smiled back to hide the jitters his expression caused.

'I did when I was training. It was a great way to spend a few days off. Many of the vineyards have cottages they rent out—total peace and serenity like this, only instead of water there are rolling hills of green vines.'

Adam's eyes were fixed on her face as if he were seeing her for the first time and the intensity of his regard seemed to burn her skin.

'I suppose it must seem a very lazy way of spending free time to someone as physically active as you,' she added lightly, wanting him to speak, to take control of things again.

'Nurses work so hard they deserve whatever degree of lethargy they can manage,' he said. He reached across and touched her lightly on the hand, then chuckled and admitted, 'I'm not always as physically active as I've been lately. I have lazy weekends where I do nothing more strenuous than read the Sunday newspapers.'

'So why—?'

He must have guessed what her question would be for he cut her off, smiling again as he said, 'It seemed like a good idea at the time. Isn't that the answer to most "why" questions?'

The waiter arrived with their first course at that moment so Sarah couldn't pursue the matter, and by the time she'd finished a delicious mixture of mango, avocado and crab in a mild chilli salsa she'd forgotten what she'd wanted to pursue.

'You'll have to try a bug,' Adam insisted, carefully removing some white meat from a char-grilled shell. 'Seeing that it's a delicacy you haven't encountered before.'

He reached across the table, fork in hand, holding the morsel of food towards her. As she closed her lips around it she glanced up and her eyes met his. Messages flashed between them, unspoken knowledge translated not into words but into feelings deep within her body,

She shivered and his fingers gently brushed her chin and pressed against her cheek, his eyes daring her to look away—or to deny what had passed between them.

For a main course she'd chosen seared tuna steaks with a lime dressing. It might have been toast and Vegemite for all she tasted, the subtle blending of flavours lost on her as she grappled with the sudden escalation of her feelings for this man she barely knew.

The attraction was physical—had been from the beginning, as far as she was concerned. In fact, tonight was the first inkling she'd had that his body might also be feeling twinges of desire.

Twinges? Who was she trying to kid?

'Would you like to see the dessert menu?'

She looked up, puzzled by his question, then glanced down and realised she'd cleaned her plate while she'd been pondering attraction.

'I don't think so,' she said, unable to avoid those dark blue eyes which beckoned and promised and tangled her in a web of desire.

'No strawberries, dipped in chocolate? I could feed them to you.'

Her heart rattled against her ribs, as if trying to break free, the image so erotic she was shaking just thinking about it.

'No!' she whispered, forcing the word out through lips aching to taste these delights—and the fingers offering them.

'A coffee?'

'Please!'

The word was more than a reply, almost an entreaty. Surely coffee would settle her jangled nerves and return some semblance of normality to the evening. She watched Adam beckon to the waiter, order coffee and murmur something else. She sat back in her chair and studied him, wondering why a night out like this should cause such an escalation in her feelings for him.

At another time—

'What are you thinking?' he asked as the waiter moved away.

She smiled, wondering, then decided it was a thought that could be shared.

'I was thinking it would be nice to have met some other way,' she said. 'Perhaps got to know each other in different circumstances.'

His eyes narrowed as if to see her more clearly, and when he spoke there was no lightness in his voice.

'Why?' he asked, making her feel foolish that she'd opened up the way she had. Perhaps he hadn't been feeling what she had. Perhaps she was imagining that this attraction was two-sided. More perhapses.

'Well, it's hardly normal circumstances, is it?' she pointed out. 'Not man and woman normal. I've arrived here with a baby you didn't know existed. You're wary, which is natural, and I'm on trial, which I understand. Whatever happens between us is likely to be judged against that background.'

She paused, hoping he'd say something or dismiss the conversation and turn it to some new subject, but he simply stared at her, his eyes darkly serious.

'Go on,' he said.

Could she?

Why not? She was a mature twenty-six-year-old, not a teenager.

'Take tonight!' Her voice was rough with the effort of speech. 'Normal would be we enjoy dinner together, you take me home, perhaps kiss—'

'Would you invite me in for coffee?'

The question startled her and she saw that he was smiling, his eyes once more a lighter blue, teasing her.

'Probably,' she admitted.

'Would I stay the night?'

Heat swept through her, so fierce and so sudden that she thought she might self-combust.

'Maybe, maybe not,' she said, trying for nonchalance but hearing the words come out like a strangled groan.

'Say it's a second date, or perhaps a third.'

The tears were so unexpected they were dribbling down her cheeks before she recognised what they were. With shaking fingers she wiped them away, and rummaged through her handbag for a handkerchief before she made a bigger fool of herself by sniffing.

He saw the moisture on her fingers and cursed himself. He'd been so caught up in the fantasy he'd pushed too hard, gone too far. Before he could apologise the waiter returned with coffee and the liqueur he'd ordered for Sarah.

'Here, try this,' he suggested. 'It's a Scotch base but I'm sure you'll like it. Guaranteed to put the miseries behind you.'

Their fingers met as he passed the glass to her, and the fire of wanting, dimmed by her sudden tears, flared anew.

'Tell me about your husband,' he said, when she'd sipped at the golden liquid, then looked up at him and half smiled as if to apologise for her sudden change of mood.

Had it been the wrong question? As the silence lengthened Adam wondered if he'd made another bad move. She set the tiny glass carefully on the table and began to talk, the huskiness of her voice accentuated by emotion.

'He was a cousin, the son of my father's cousin. I'd known him all my life—growing up in the country on neighbouring properties, holidaying together. We were married when I was eighteen. It united the family business our great-grandfather had founded so the families were overjoyed.'

Did you love him? The words burned on his tongue but remained unsaid. He'd had enough trouble with his questions this evening.

'Eighteen months later we came down to the beach for summer holidays. My parents, Colin and I. We spent Christmas and New Year there, but when it was time to go back I stayed on. I had a wisdom tooth coming through. It had given me trouble on and off for a while so I'd made an appointment to see the dentist. Colin was to fly back down the following weekend to take me home.'

Her cool emotional voice and the echo of her words— 'I have no family'—told him all he needed to know. He signalled to the waiter and slipped him a credit card, silently indicating he wanted to pay and leave. Then he reached across the table and took Sarah's hand, holding her fingers tightly as she gazed blankly out over the stretch of water and finished what she'd begun.

'The plane crashed. They were all killed. The investigation failed to find a reason. Colin had been flying since he was sixteen—had his pilot's licence before his driver's. Six months later I started training as a nurse.'

She looked up at him, smudges of fatigue shadowing her lovely eyes.

'I had to do something,' she said, and the grief she must have felt, the total sense of loss, gripped at his intestines, crushing them like a tightening fist.

The waiter returned and Adam signed the account. Still holding her hand, he stood. He could understand why Sam was so important to her now—he was the family she'd lost—but he knew this wasn't the moment to say that—especially as he wasn't at all certain he'd be able to sign the baby away. Where Sam was concerned he now had the problem of affection added to the bonds of family plus the feelings and emotional needs of his mother and grandmother.

He held Sarah close as they left the restaurant, and knew from the way her body nestled into his that she appreciated the contact. Had there been boyfriends in the years between then and now—men in her life? Surely there had been, yet if she'd been in a relationship would she have taken Fiona in and devoted her life to someone else's child?

As they reached the car she straightened and moved away from him, turning to face him as he opened the door for her. A smile hovered on her lips and the moonlight turned her eyes to the colour of pewter.

'It was a lovely evening,' she said, with the formal politeness of a well-brought-up child. 'I'm sorry I cast gloom over it like that.'

Adam sucked in air and held it in his lungs. He knew that what came next would be important, perhaps vital, to their relationship, although he wasn't certain why.

'I feel honoured you told me,' he said quietly, and the

tremulous smile became real, the flat sheen of pewter-coloured eyes transformed by silver sparks. Was it the smile that made him kiss her then? The way her lips tilted and invited?

Hours later, lying sleepless in a bed which had suddenly become lumpy and uncomfortable and very large for one, he worried over it. At the time it had seemed to be the logical thing to do—to take her in his arms and taste the promise of those lips.

And she'd kissed him back. There was no mistaking that. She'd kissed him with a passion that had burnt through to his toes. Her body had been soft, curving into his, the bones he'd felt before so fragile that he'd longed to keep her safe within his arms for ever.

As standing-up-in-car-parks kisses went, it hadn't been bad. In fact, it had been a boomer. He stared at the ceiling and remembered the way she'd smiled at him as they'd pulled apart, looking only at each other—not at the young, insensitive lout who'd wolf-whistled at them.

'A bit silly, choosing this place when there's so much moonlight and water around,' she'd said, her slightly swollen, well-kissed lips curling into a smile. It had made him want to start all over again, beginning with the dimple in her cheek.

'There's moonlight and water back home,' he'd said temptingly, and had seen a different expression flash across her face. Had it been regret?

'There's also a baby and all the problems we had before we started kissing,' she reminded him. Then she'd put out her hand in a formal gesture and said, 'Thank you for a lovely evening.'

It had told him immediately that the night was over—no invitation to come in for coffee after this dinner date.

*   *   *

Sarah was surprised to find him in the living area, slumped on a comfortable chair reading the paper, when she went down to fix breakfast for herself and Sam next morning. She tried not to notice how much the faded denim shirt suited him or the way his thigh muscles moved as he shifted in the chair, dropping the paper on the floor and holding out his arms towards Sam.

Determined to keep her distance, Sarah set Sam down on the floor and watched him crawl towards Adam. Sam didn't know about sliced bread yet, but if he had he'd certainly have put Adam above it on his list of 'best things'.

She mixed his cereal, put toast on for herself, poured juice into a trainer mug and wondered what to do next.

'I'll feed him,' Adam offered, which meant, of course, that she had to go closer to him—within touching distance yet—in order to give him the food.

'I thought you were going hiking or rock-climbing this weekend,' she said, setting food and drink on the coffee-table in front of him and retreating behind the kitchen bar again.

'Changed my mind,' he said laconically—so laconically she looked suspiciously at him. He'd *never* sounded that laid-back before!

'Well, what will you do?' she demanded.

'Hang about, I suppose. What do you do at the weekend?'

She shrugged.

'Take Sam to the beach. During the day when the sun's warm he can play in the shallows. Do the washing, go for a walk, read a book while he's sleeping.'

As she reeled off her weekend pursuits they sounded dreary. Back home, after she'd given up work, the days hadn't been as neatly delineated into week-days and weekends, but she'd enjoyed her life—every day of it. Hadn't she?

Not that Adam noticed her distraction. He was busy feeding Sam and not finding it as easy as it looked.

'Sit still, you brat.' Sam smiled at him and waved his fists in appreciation of the compliment. Adam looked across at Sarah. 'First thing this morning I'll go and hire a chair for him. A high chair, did you call it? Are some better than others? Perhaps you should come.'

Sarah sighed. Of course she should go. There were only a few brands and designs of high chairs she'd allow Sam to sit in, not trusting the stability of the others. But doing something as mundane as hiring a high chair was dangerously like a family thing to do—seductive in its appeal, impossible in reality.

Was that his idea? Had he cancelled his weekend plans so he could torment her with this image of family—two parents sharing the caring? Whether planned or not, that's what happened. She had to endure the sight of him reaching for Sam as the waves threatened to tumble the chubby body over in the shallow water, and Sam riding high on the broad shoulders, shouting his delight to the sky.

Worse torment was the full-on proximity of Adam's body and the lustful response of her own. Every time he moved, stretched, spread himself beside her on a towel on the beach or sat down across the kitchen bar her body reacted, wanting to feel the muscle, touch the sun-warmed skin, brush the droplets of water from his hair. It was as if he held her captive in an invisible cage, removed from the real world by her own desire.

She loved and hated every waking minute—praying for the weekend to be over, praying for it to last for ever. Her head knew the dangers. It told her incessantly that to give in to this attraction would be sheer stupidity. From her side there'd be heartache when she left. Although she knew she could cope with the aftermath of any disaster, it was Adam's reaction that had her worried.

A double-edged sword was poised above her head. Adam, suspicion still lurking in his heart, would be sure to see any capitulation on her part as a ploy to get the letter signed. Add to that the question of whether he'd be willing to sign over his nephew to a woman who indulged in casual affairs, and she was in a no-win situation.

So she chatted and pretended and told herself it was better this way, while her body ached with longings she'd never felt before and her head ached with the constant reiteration of 'be sensible' warnings.

He'd lost her, Adam realised as he sat on the beach on Sunday afternoon with Sam at his feet, watching as she steered his old surfboard along the crest of a wave, her lovely body so beautifully balanced she seemed at one with the ocean. Although the car-park kiss had told him the attraction he felt for her wasn't one-sided, the formal handshake had been a declaration that she wasn't going to do one damn thing about it.

He'd hoped that if he hung around all weekend, putting himself through torture like he'd never known before, he might have had an opportunity to get close to her again, to break through the barrier of reserve she'd built around her like an invisible cage.

By the time Sarah came in, the board lifted easily to her shoulders, her body dripping with water and her eyes shining with delight, the inaction and frustration had built up to such a pitch he knew he had to find some release. He carried the board back up to the house but left his visitors on the beach. His mind blanked against any argument, he phoned a friend, arranged a game of squash, then rang one of the women he saw occasionally and invited her out to dinner.

'Been stood up by the woman you were kissing in Grumpy's car park?' Lorena asked. 'From the way that looked, I thought I'd have to cross you off my list of useful men.'

'Do you want to eat with me or not?' he growled, regretting the phone call even more than the kiss.

Lorena agreed so he changed quickly into his squash gear, found some better clothes for going out later and hurried down the stairs, hoping to escape before Sarah and Sam returned. There was no sign of her in the living area so he left a note to explain he'd be out to dinner and slunk quietly out of his own house, feeling both shame and anger.

As Adam drove them to the clinic on Monday Sarah realised it was as if Friday had never been—or that was the way Adam had decided to play it. They were back to being colleagues, and not particularly friendly ones. It was a relief, she told herself. Although his body hadn't lost any of its magnetism towards hers, it was easier for her to handle the brisk, no-nonsense boss than the seductive friend he'd played on Friday evening.

Tuesday, Wednesday and Thursday morning all passed with a minimum of contact outside the treatment room. Sarah and Sam ate their dinners alone, Adam being out exercising something somewhere. It should have made things easier, but it didn't. If anything, it exacerbated the tension between them, stringing Sarah's nerves so tightly she felt the slightest twitch might make her shatter.

Returning from a quick lunch and shopping expedition, she looked in on Sam and Jacinta who were playing in the gym, then went out to relieve Jane at the reception desk. Adam was there and Sarah watched Jane hang up the phone and turn to him.

'You've got a celebrity patient coming in,' she said 'One of the golf professionals, playing on the international circuit, no less. He's here for the tournament at Sanctuary Cove later this week.'

Adam whistled when Jane gave the man's name.

'I thought he'd have his own doctor among his entourage—or physio at the very least. Did he say what's wrong?'

'He didn't phone—one of his assistants made the call. Said it was his wrist, a recurring problem. He wants a cortisone injection.'

'Stop the pain and keep on going,' Adam muttered. 'If these people stuck with strengthening exercises they'd be so much better off. They all know they can only have so much cortisone each year.' He glanced at Sarah then turned back to Jane. 'Can you dig out a sheet of forearm-strengthening exercises? Sarah, you study it while I'm seeing him then we'll take him into the treatment room and go through them together. You'll have to do the exercises to show him what I want.'

'Back to bossy mode,' Sarah said, watching his retreating back and thinking how she'd miss that sight, no matter how bossy he was.

'Been bad all week,' Jane agreed, and gave Sarah the look which said she could keep her mouth shut if Sarah wanted to tell her what was going on.

Sarah grinned at her and shook her head.

'Nothing to do with me,' she said, although that was probably a lie.

The conversation went no further, interrupted by the arrival of the 'real' patient—a man whose face was so familiar to Sarah from newspaper and TV she had to fight an urge to greet him like an old friend. Not that he was the kind of man she'd want for a friend if all the newspaper reports were anywhere near correct. And surely some of it must be true—no reporter would make up so long a string of ex-wives and lovers.

Jane diverted her thoughts, slapping a sheet of paper in front of her, before she flashed a charming smile at the patient.

'Good morning, sir. If you'd come this way?' she said sweetly, and ushered him towards Adam's door.

Sarah studied the exercises. They seemed simple enough, but the last required equipment—a round stick like a broom handle, with a weight on a long piece of string tied in the middle of it. Had she seen something like that in the treatment room? Where?

Among the conditions these exercises would help was medial epicondylitis. Great! Just what I've always wanted to have, she thought, then was pleased to find an explanation, following the grand-sounding complaint— torn tendons where the forearm flexor muscles attached to the bone. It was reasonably common among golfers, baseball pitchers, tennis and squash players—anyone who used a lot of wrist rotation in their sport.

Rotating her wrist experimentally, she felt the move- ment which could cause the trouble. Obeying the orders on the sheet, she sat in a chair and rested her forearm on the arm-rest. If she tried all the exercises herself now, she'd be less likely to make a fool of herself later.

The first strengthening exercise was squeezing a rubber ball or rubber baton in the hand. She could do that one, no trouble. The next was just as simple.

Supporting her forearm on the arm-rest, with her palm facing downwards, she had to raise her hand and lower it as far as possible both ways. Then, turning her arm over but still supporting the forearm, she had to repeat the exercises in the new position. The next was harder and she pitied anyone who had to try it with a wrist already painful.

By the time Adam called her she'd gone through the list three times, had found the stick with string and weight and was confident she could demonstrate all the exercises effectively.

'Ah, at last, a pretty woman come to rescue me,' the golfer greeted her. He acknowledged Adam's introduction with another compliment and Sarah smiled.

'You sit here,' Adam said to his patient, biting off the words so they sounded like an order. 'Sarah, you demonstrate while I move the injured wrist.'

She obeyed, although his attitude surprised her. True, from what she had seen of Adam, she wouldn't have expected him to kowtow to anyone, no matter how famous. But she'd have thought he'd use the man's name, show some degree of courtesy to any patient.

Not that the golfer seemed to notice anything amiss. He continued to flirt with Sarah as she demonstrated the exercises, making her smile with his glib remarks and teasing comments.

'I thought women objected to that kind of behaviour these days—couldn't it be classed as sexual harassment?' Adam growled when he returned from seeing the man out and found Sarah, disposing of the swab and needle from the cortisone injection.

She faced him, surprised by the aggression in his voice.

'It was harmless banter,' she assured him. 'The man probably has a supply of it for every known situation.'

'You laughed and smiled—played up to him.' He accompanied the accusation with a scowl. 'I suppose all women do because he's famous.'

'If I laughed and smiled it's because he was amusing, which is more than can be said for some people,' Sarah retorted. 'And I would think it's because he's so well known he uses it to protect himself. It's like conversational armour, a verbal façade, so he doesn't have to bare his real self to all the thousands of people he meets and has to be polite to each year.'

Silence greeted her words—an uneasy silence which she felt obliged to break.

'Besides, according to the gossip columns, he's between wives at the moment and you did say I should have a husband.'

Adam glared at her, aware she was teasing him but unable to respond in kind.

'If I thought for one moment you were serious there'd be no more talk of you adopting Sam.'

'Oh, lighten up!' Sarah suggested, realising she'd gone too far and hiding the fear that was stabbing at her heart. 'It was a joke. As if a man like that would look twice at a mousy thing like me. And as if I'd want him. There's more to life than lots of money.'

She spun on her heel and marched out of the room.

He'd heard the anger in her voice, but in the last sentence there'd been bitterness as well. He found himself wanting to protest about the 'mousy' description, and to ask her what she did consider important in life. But he was angry too, but in a different way—with himself for reacting so strongly to the man's flirting, with Sarah for disrupting his life to the extent where he could no longer think straight.

She'd been here over a fortnight and he still had no idea what he should do. He accepted that Sam was his nephew and, having done that, could he let anyone adopt him? Could he bring himself to sign away this child of Fiona's?

He rather doubted he could so why was he letting this woman think he might? Why was he insisting she stayed on here, giving her false hope that he might agree to the adoption? Was it for some agenda of his own? And, if and when he did refuse, where would that leave Sarah? Devastated, that's where! Probably grief-stricken as well. Could he do it to her?

He had to get this sorted out, start finding answers instead of more questions. Now!

Sarah regretted her hasty departure. Had she jeopardised her chances, snapping at him as she had?

Well, it was his fault. He unsettled her. He'd been unsettling her all week. And he kept looking at her when he didn't think she was watching, his eyes soft, both puzzled and puzzling, some other message—maybe sexual—lurking in the ocean-blue depths.

CHAPTER TEN

By Friday morning Adam had a plan—complicated, intricate, confusing even, but still a plan.

'Would you come into my office as soon as you've settled Sam with Jacinta?' he said to Sarah as they were getting out of the car at the clinic.

She looked at him, her eyes so wary he wanted to say, 'Hey, don't worry—it's good, not bad'. But he couldn't do that because he wasn't certain how she'd take any of this.

Sarah did as she was told and settled Sam, then walked down the corridor to his office. Her legs ached with tension, instinct telling her this was a showdown of some kind. She tapped on his door and entered when he responded. He waved her towards the chair she'd sat in that first day, though he wasn't beside her this time but across the desk—official!

She looked at his face—expressionless. His eyes—hooded by lashes as dark as soot.

'Here's the letter you wanted,' he said, and passed her a piece of paper.

No! Her heart cried out in protest, although she knew it was what she'd come for—what she'd wanted more than anything else in the world.

Why did her hands refuse to take it? Why did she feel as if she'd lost, not won? Why was such utter devastation chilling her soul?

'Thank you.' Upbringing forced the traditional reply,

170

but although he'd put the paper on the desk in front of her she couldn't pick it up.

'There are no conditions. No ifs, or buts or maybes,' he assured her. 'It simply says you have my blessing to adopt Sam. I had it notarised so it's a legal document.'

'Thank you,' she said again, aware of the phrase's inadequacy but unable to form any other words. Her lips and throat were as dry as tinder and her heartbeat so erratic she was surprised she hadn't passed out.

She lifted the letter and folded it carefully, pressing her cold, stiff fingers along each crease to prolong the moment when she had to get out of the chair and make her way out the door. Would her legs hold her up or would she stagger like a drunk? That's how she felt— as disorientated as any drunk!

When the paper was a smaller and very neatly folded rectangle she glanced up to find him watching her, his face as blankly uninformative as she'd ever seen it.

'I'll make arrangements to go home,' she said, and pushed herself to her feet.

She made it to the door—didn't stagger at all—but all the way she waited for him to call her back, to say something—anything.

He waited until she had her hand on the doorknob before he said quietly, 'If that's what you want to do.'

It was unanswerable. She could hardly spin towards him and shout that, no, it wasn't what she wanted to do. He'd obviously decided she'd outstayed her welcome. She stumbled to the lunch-room, tucked the piece of paper carefully into her handbag and went through to the gym where her swimmers had gathered.

Her swimmers? Not for much longer! Perhaps she should move to a hotel until she could get on a train.

No, it would upset Sam—another move before they undertook the lengthy journey.

'You with us?' Jake called to her, and she set her misery aside and concentrated on her tasks—normal stretching for flexibility then ballistic stretching exercises, attempting to encourage the participants' shoulders beyond the normal range of movements. Fast movements, counting to keep them sharp and co-ordinated, as she tried not to think of Adam or his sudden decision and dismissal.

Richard phoned while she was minding the reception desk at lunchtime. Adam had gone out, telling her he wouldn't be back but that he'd arranged for Jacinta to drive her home.

'And I won't be in tonight,' he'd added, just before he disappeared.

'So, what's new?' she'd muttered at the closing door, then she picked up the receiver.

'It's not a big party, maybe twenty friends. To celebrate my retirement from football. I thought you might like to come.'

She hesitated. Richard had been in four times and she now strapped his shoulder herself. He was a likeable man, easy and diverting company, and if ever she'd needed diverting it was today.

'I've got Sam,' she objected, 'and no transport.'

'Get a babysitter and a cab,' he ordered. 'I won't take no for an answer. If you don't arrive by eight o'clock I'll have to leave my own party and fetch you myself.'

Sarah was surprised to find herself smiling.

'Give me the address. I'll be there,' she promised, the smile lighting a small glow of excitement in her internal gloom.

Jacinta was happy to babysit, and with that assurance and Jane's return to man the reception desk Sarah took herself off to the now-familiar shopping mall. There was a dress in a boutique window there which had been calling to her for some time.

The small glow grew, making her wonder how long it had been since she'd bought herself something special. If she could keep her mind on superficial things, like clothes and Richard's party, perhaps she could ignore the ache of despair in her chest.

The dress was just as lovely as she'd remembered it—a light, filmy georgette with an asymmetrically layered skirt, which flirted around her knees, and a fitted bodice. The material was a peachy cream, splashed with roses of pale pink, deepening to watermelon. It was ultra-feminine, and when she tried it on the colour enhanced the golden tan she'd acquired and made her face look less pale.

She studied her reflection, and regretted that Adam wouldn't see her in it.

That was the past! She'd put other things behind her so she could with this, she mentally told her image.

Sheer stockings and new lacy underwear completed her purchases and she hurried back to work, feeling, if not excited, at least alive again.

Even Sam seemed to understand her need for this evening of freedom and went quietly to bed and straight off to sleep, allowing her to take her time as she dressed and applied her make-up. She refused to think of the excitement she'd felt a week ago as she'd prepared to go out with Adam, dressing in the hope she'd knock his socks off—even if she hadn't let that particular wish form as a coherent thought.

Tonight the only socks available to be knocked off were those of Richard and a few of his footballing friends, but her ego demanded she looked her best.

His house was a low, sprawling building on the bank of one of the area's many canals. From the noise level, it seemed that many of the guests had already arrived.

Richard greeted her with a whistle of appreciation.

'Come through,' he said, taking her by the hand. 'We're all out the back by the canal—gathered around the barbecue like at any good Aussie party. I'll introduce you around then I'll have to cook, but if anyone gives you any trouble I won't be far away.'

'Out the back' was a beautiful outdoor entertaining area, with a terracotta-tiled floor and a vine-covered pergola providing shelter. Mingling with the smell of the fire was the delicate perfume of some sweet night-scented jasmine.

The guests stood in groups or lounged against the pergola pillars. Everyone was welcoming. Some of the women complimented her on her dress, others asked questions about the west and the men asked how long she might stay. Richard stayed by her side, excusing them after a few minutes to take her to the next cluster of people.

'Shouldn't you be cooking something?' she asked, when he led her further along the wide patio.

'One more chap to meet,' he said. 'I kept him till last because I thought you and he might hit it off. He's with the noisy lot up the end here.'

So much for bodily awareness! Sarah, edged into the small group by Richard's persistence, was face to face with Adam before she realised he was there. With a mammoth effort she acknowledged the other guests as

Richard introduced them, and acknowledged Adam, too, as Richard said his name.

She answered questions about her home state, fielded compliments on her dress, explained she wasn't over on this side of Australia for long and generally kept up her end of the conversation quite credibly—she thought.

Richard disappeared, returning to press a cold drink into her hand. 'I've got to get back to the fire,' he said to no one in particular, and disappeared again.

Adam said something to the man beside him and, whether prompted by his remark or coincidentally, the other members of the group drifted away, leaving Sarah and Adam alone in the scented shadows.

'Are we going to keep up this pretence of not knowing each other?' Sarah demanded, using anger to batten down her inner excitement.

'I think so,' he said smoothly. 'Didn't you say something about if we'd met under different circumstances? Richard has kindly provided the different circumstances—couldn't we at least see what comes of it?'

He didn't sound as certain as he usually did but she wasn't going to be swayed by a little uncertainty. She clung to her anger.

'You connived with Richard—arranged all this to set me up.'

He took a step to narrow the distance between them, coming within touching range.

'Not to set you up but to meet you as we might have met had fate been less capricious. To talk to you, begin to get to know you, perhaps offer you a lift home...'

Her anger was dissolving in the fizzy bubbles of excitement, rising in its place.

'Would you expect to be invited in for coffee?' she

asked, clinging to the remnants of common sense now that anger had deserted her.

He smiled at her, that devastating smile which coiled deep into her lungs, setting them aflutter and her heart jiggling again.

'That's up to you,' he said, then he looked deep into her eyes and added, 'I mean it, Sarah. It *is* up to you. Sam's yours now so there's no hidden agenda here, no questions in either of our minds. Let's move on to what might be in our hearts.'

He heard the words but could hardly believe he'd said them and felt a clutch of fear. He'd wagered all on this last throw of the dice—not only what he felt for Sarah but his future relationship with Sam now hung in the balance.

'And the compliments you've already received don't begin to describe how beautiful you look this evening. In fact, when I saw you walk in I was jealous you'd dressed that way for Richard and not for me.'

He studied her face, trying to find some reaction there. Her eyes gleamed like pools of silver, the play of light and shade highlighting the fine bones of her face, but he couldn't discern her expression.

He tried another smile and an uneasy half-shrug. He moistened his lips, took a deep breath for luck, then blurted out his thoughts, letting them tumble over each other the way her words had that first day they'd met.

'Hell, Sarah, you might help me out here. Am I doing OK or not? I've said flowery things to women before, paid compliments as sincere, but I've never felt all knotted up, wondering if they believed me or not. I know we haven't known each other long, but I was attracted to you from the beginning and now I think—I'm nearly sure, in fact—that I've fallen in love with you.'

He paused hopefully and saw the beginnings of a smile, dancing at the corner of her lips.

'What do you need to do so you'd know for certain—or will "nearly sure" do?' she asked, the dimple, which had begun to fascinate him when he'd first set eyes on her, pressing into her cheek.

He touched the indentation with his forefinger.

'A kiss might help.' He breathed the words, his chest so tight with hope it felt as if a giant vice was wedged around his ribs.

The dimple fluttered beneath his finger. She took a step towards him and raised her head. Her eyes met his, then closed. He felt the brush of her lips across his mouth, teasing him before fitting more closely and persuading his into a response.

Not that it took much persuasion. His body was racing ahead of his mind. His arms worked independently and drew her close, fitting her to him. His fingers tangled in her hair, his lips tasting her sweetness—and the promise of hope.

'If you two keep that up much longer someone will throw a bucket of water over you.'

Richard's warning broke them guiltily apart. Well, not quite apart. Their fingers clung together and other bits of their bodies brushed against each other for physical reassurance that the miracle of love was alive and well between them.

'Come and join the party,' Richard insisted, and reluctantly they followed him towards the noise and other guests.

Sarah felt the tension in Adam's fingers, even stronger than her own, and realised how unsettled, perhaps uncertain, he still was, even after a kiss.

'I will invite you in for coffee,' she whispered to him.

His hand gripped hers more tightly for an instant then relaxed. He smiled down at her, his eyes brimming with excitement.

They spent the evening side by side, at times joining in the general conversation and at other times sitting a little apart to talk to each other—to explore and learn a little of each other's pasts. Inevitably, the talk turned to Fiona for it was she who, however inadvertently, had brought them together.

'I worked in midwifery at the public hospital,' Sarah explained, 'and was running an exercise class for expectant women. Fiona turned up there one day, thin but obviously pregnant.'

She paused, not wanting to hurt the man she loved but knowing he'd want to know.

'She was devastated by the pregnancy, yet kind of happy and excited at the same time—a little high perhaps. I think she'd have had to have been to show up at the hospital. After the others left we talked and something clicked between us.'

Adam nodded as if he understood.

'I asked her where she was living and she waved towards the door and muttered something about a squat and friends. I got the impression she wasn't happy there—why would she be? Somehow I ended up asking her if she'd like to stay with me until the baby was born.'

'And she never talked about her family—told you what had started her on drugs?'

Sarah shook her head, sorry she couldn't ease the pain for Adam.

'I knew she came from over here originally and also knew she had regrets—not only about the drugs but about many other things. It was as if they heaped themselves on her back and left her old and bowed before her time. It seemed that when she was high she could throw them off, but the moment the potency wore off they'd be back, pressing down even more heavily than before.'

She paused, remembering Fiona, then found one gift she could offer to this man. 'But when she was high she was such fun, Adam, a truly lovely person with so much joy and zest. I had to wonder what had happened in her life to steal it all away so she had to find relief, oblivion, in chemical dreams.'

He took her hand in his and held it tightly.

'She was sixteen, just learning to drive. My father had to visit an old friend up in the hinterland and he took Fiona along as it was an opportunity for her to practise on less crowded roads. Like your family's accident, we'll never know for certain what happened because afterwards she had no recollection of it. We can only assume she swerved to avoid an animal, a wallaby or wombat, lost control of the car and that was it. My father was killed. Fiona blamed herself, and in spite of all the counselling we could provide—no matter how much love and assurance we pressed on her—she lost her ability to cope.'

Adam's voice, as he spoke, was tight with pain. Sarah clung to his fingers, aware of the uselessness of words but offering silent comfort and understanding.

'I told myself back then I'd never get too close to another human being,' he admitted, turning to look into Sarah's eyes so she could read the truth and see his love. 'Then you sneaked in under my guard, you and Sam.'

She smiled, accepting what she saw and warming to it.

'So it's really Sam you want?' she teased. 'That's what this big effort's all about?'

'Sam and his mother,' he answered, his voice so husky with desire she felt it ripple down her spine.

'Perhaps we should go home for coffee,' she suggested, and saw the love change to desire, flickering in the blue depths like phosphorescence in the midnight-darkened ocean.

'You're supposed to be helping yourselves to food. I'll have coffee here later,' Richard complained, his voice breaking into the net of togetherness they'd woven about themselves. Politeness forced them to stay, and playing at the party game heightened their hunger for each other.

Sarah told him of her family, of the properties she'd inherited from her parents and Colin, the vineyard she'd not mentioned the night they'd gone to dinner.

'They all have very competent managers on them, but having an income made it possible to leave work to care for Fiona and later Sam.' She hesitated, then admitted, 'It was to make sure Sam had a future that I wanted to adopt him. My lawyer told me I could make him my beneficiary in my will but distant cousins would be less likely to contest it if he was my legal child.'

'You wanted to adopt Sam so you could leave him untold wealth, and I treated you like a woman trying to sell me the Sydney Harbour bridge?'

She chuckled at the simile.

'It's not untold wealth, but I'm comfortably off,' she protested.

'You would be,' he said gloomily. 'Now you're going to think I'm marrying you for your money.'

'And are you?' she prompted.

'Marrying you for your money? Most definitely not!'

She grinned at his indignant denial.

'I wasn't talking about the money but the marrying

bit,' she murmured, snuggling closer to him as excitement squirmed inside her.

'I haven't asked?'

He hit his forehead with the palm of his hand.

'Come on, we've done polite. Let's get out of here.'

They'd barely pulled away from Richard's drive when Adam stopped the car and leaned across to take her in his arms.

'Will you marry me?' he demanded, and, not waiting for an answer, added, 'Soon?'

He kissed her with an intensity that pledged his love as no words could, then he lifted his head and spoke again.

'Will you have to go home? Settle any business? Will you like living here or would you prefer to move? My mother and grandmother are here, but we could all move to the west if that's what you wanted. They'll be home on Monday and could help me mind Sam if you wanted to fly over or I could take time off and fly with you and they could mind Sam—'

'Hey!' Sarah shifted so she could press her lips against his to stop the flow. 'I'm the one who stumbles over words when I'm confused. Do you want answers to all those questions right now or would one answer do to go on with and we'll sort out the rest as we go along?'

He chuckled and drew her close, resting his chin on her head.

'One answer will do for now as long as it's yes,' he said quietly. 'Anything else is unimportant at the moment. Will you marry me, Sarah Tremayne?'

'Yes, Adam,' she whispered, and wondered at the feeling of completeness the simple declaration gave her.

EPILOGUE

SARAH felt the first twinge of pain as she set up the bassinet in the corner of their bedroom. It was a woven cane basket which fitted on a stand, gleaming with the new coat of white paint Adam had finished seven months ago. Next time she wouldn't tell him she was pregnant until at least three months. Within forty-eight hours of her last announcement he'd gone rummaging through his mother's store-room, unearthing relics of his and Fiona's past and bringing them home proudly like offerings to lay at her feet.

She smiled at the thought, looking out the window to where he sat on the beach, watching Sam, now a sturdy two-year-old, racing in and out of the water. The next contraction came as she was tucking sheets around the mattress—brand new, the mattress, but the sheets had been her own, and her father's and grandfather's before her. They'd been kept in a trunk of her mother's precious things, carefully hand-stitched and embroidered by a woman on a dry and dusty cattle property in the far north-west of Australia over a hundred years ago.

She pressed her hand against the ache below the bulge in her stomach and waited for the next contraction, knowing there was plenty of time to do what had to be done, finishing her preparations in the room that had been hers and Sam's when they'd first come to this house. Adam had willingly given up his eyrie in the sky—for a while at least—until the children were older and wouldn't need attention in the night.

He'd given up so much, Sarah thought, to spend more time with her and Sam, to bond them into a family.

She walked down the steps, good exercise, checked the fridge and freezer—although she knew there was enough food to withstand a siege of several months—then phoned her mother-in-law.

'No, I haven't told him yet,' she said. 'I keep thinking of his state when Maggie went into labour. I'd like to postpone his reaction for as long as possible. Maybe he'll guess when he sees you and Grandma here.'

He didn't! He came in cheerfully from the beach, bathed and dressed Sam then settled him for a nap, carrying on as if nothing untoward was happening. He was delighted, as ever, to have his maternal relatives visiting, but even when they stayed for dinner he made no comment, apart from expressing pleasure in their company.

'Some doctor,' his mother said, when he turned off the television at ten-thirty and suggested they all headed off to bed.

'What do you mean—"some doctor"?' Adam demanded. He looked surprised as the three women laughed at him.

'Your wife's been in the early stages of labour since one o'clock,' his grandmother explained. They all laughed again as he stared at her, then at his mother and finally allowed his gaze to come to rest on his extremely pregnant wife.

'You didn't tell me!' he gasped. Sarah wondered if she should have brought some oxygen home from the surgery. He was hyperventilating so badly he could have used it.

'I thought I'd wait until as late as possible,' she said, smiling up at him as he held her in his arms and looked down into her face with total anguish. 'Although I would have thought a man who can pick up a twinge of pain in an athlete a hundred yards away might have noticed I was suffering a little discomfort at quite regular intervals.'

'I didn't— You couldn't— We—' His words were as disjointed as his movements.

'It's OK, Adam. It had to happen eventually, you know,' she assured him, patting his cheek and smoothing the worry lines that creased his forehead.

'Can you remember what to do?' he demanded, and she chuckled.

'Most of it comes naturally, I'm told.'

'No—what *I* do,' he muttered. 'I went to all those classes and now I can't remember a damned thing. What do I do? When do you breathe and when do you pant?'

Sarah stood on tiptoe and with a great deal of difficulty, given her stomach and discomfort, reached up to kiss his lips.

'Just be there for me,' she said. 'That's all you have to do.'

He wasn't satisfied or appeased. He fussed over her and fretted over his inability to remember, hurling instructions at his mother for the care of Sam and searching desperately for his car keys.

'I think I'll ring Richard and get him to drive me in,' Sarah teased, handing him the car keys, taking his squash bag out of his hands and replacing it with the bag she'd packed for hospital.

'No, no, I'm doing fine,' he protested, urging her into the lift although she felt the stairs might help to hurry things along.

With infinite tenderness he helped her into the car, strapping her in with trembling hands. He got in himself and was about to do up his seat belt when he obviously remembered something.

'We haven't told Sam!' he said. 'He doesn't know.'

Sarah reached out and took his hand.

'Your mother will tell Sam when he wakes up in the morning. Two-year-olds don't need progress reports.'

'Progress reports! I haven't got the numbers of all the people I want to phone as soon as it's born.'

She remembered his procrastination when Maggie had been about to deliver and tightened her grip on his fingers.

'I'll look them up for you when we get there,' she promised. 'Now, unless you want to deliver your child in the garage here, I suggest you get me to the hospital as soon as possible.'

He stopped arguing, merely going a deathly white and making four attempts to get the engine going before it finally fired. Then he forgot to open the garage doors, before rolling forward.

'I should have driven,' Sarah muttered to herself, pressing the remote so the doors opened just enough for the car to slide under them as they headed for the street. 'Or taken a cab.'

They made it to the highway without incident, but when Adam stopped at a green traffic light she wondered if it would be better to get out right there and walk the rest of the way.

'I didn't phone the doctor!' he spluttered, oblivious to the blaring hooters of late night motorists. 'That's what I had to do. It was on the list. I didn't bring the list.'

'I phoned the doctor—now drive!' Sarah told him, the situation becoming less humorous as the pains increased in intensity and frequency.

At the hospital a kindly woman, obviously used to

dealing with demented fathers, took care of Adam while Sarah checked in and followed a nurse to the birthing suites.

It was familiar yet unfamiliar—the atmosphere more pampered than where she'd trained and worked, the pain and jokes the same. She was aware of Adam by her side but thought of Fiona when the time came to deliver, and later named the baby for the woman who had given her so much.

'It wasn't so bad,' Adam told his mother when the whole family was gathered next morning to examine the tiny black-haired girl Sarah cradled in her arms. 'And I'll do even better next time.'

'Next time?' Sarah echoed. 'Who said anything about a next time? I don't know that I can go through it again.'

He bent towards her, taking her free hand in his, his face creased with concern.

'I'm sorry, darling. That was insensitive of me. You're the one who suffered all the pain.'

She grinned at him.

'It wasn't the pain I won't go through again,' she said, resting her cheek on the downy little head and smiling at Sam who was so fascinated by the baby he was both still and quiet. 'It was your behaviour. Next baby, you can go west to check on our investments when I'm due. Sam would have been more help than you!'

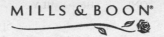

MILLS & BOON®

Makes
any time
special

Enjoy a romantic novel from
Mills & Boon®

Presents™ Enchanted™ Temptation

Historical Romance™ Medical Romance™

MILLS & BOON®

Medical Romance™

COMING NEXT MONTH

A TRUSTWORTHY MAN by Josie Metcalfe

Sister Abigail Walker thoroughly enjoyed her work in the A&E department, even more so when Dr Ben Taylor arrived! But was Ben the trustworthy and gentle colleague she thought him to be…

BABIES ON HER MIND by Jessica Matthews

Midwife Emily Chandler had not intended to succumb to obstetrician Will Patton. Just because she found herself unexpectedly pregnant was no reason to marry him but Will had other ideas!

OUR NEW MUMMY by Jennifer Taylor
A Country Practice—the second of four books.

Dr David Ross was unprepared for his reaction to the arrival of Laura Mackenzie, consultant paediatrician. Was he betraying the memory of his wife or was it time to move on…

TIME ENOUGH by Carol Wood

Dr Ben Buchan's new locum, Dr Kate Ross, was making a determined effort to start her life again. But did that include becoming involved with the boss?

Available from 4th June 1999

Available at most branches of WH Smith, Tesco, Asda, Martins, Borders, Easons, Volume One/James Thin and most good paperback bookshops

FREE

2 Books
and a surprise gift!

We would like to take this opportunity to thank you for reading this Mills & Boon® book by offering you the chance to take TWO more specially selected titles from the Medical Romance™ series absolutely FREE! We're also making this offer to introduce you to the benefits of the Reader Service™ —

- ★ FREE home delivery
- ★ FREE gifts and competitions
- ★ FREE monthly Newsletter
- ★ Books available before they're in the shops
- ★ Exclusive Reader Service discounts

Accepting these FREE books and gift places you under no obligation to buy; you may cancel at any time, even after receiving your free shipment. Simply complete your details below and return the entire page to the address below. *You don't even need a stamp!*

YES! Please send me 2 free Medical Romance books and a surprise gift. I understand that unless you hear from me, I will receive 4 superb new titles every month for just £2.40 each, postage and packing free. I am under no obligation to purchase any books and may cancel my subscription at any time. The free books and gift will be mine to keep in any case.

M9EB

Ms/Mrs/Miss/Mr ....Initials...

BLOCK CAPITALS PLEASE

Surname...

Address...

....

....Postcode ....

Send this whole page to:
THE READER SERVICE, FREEPOST CN81, CROYDON, CR9 3WZ
(Eire readers please send coupon to: P.O. Box 4546, Dublin 24.)